THE FAILSAFE PROGRAM

AN ALAN HARRISON AND LAYLA NOVEL

J E SUTTON JR

HEARTSTONE PRESS

JS HEARTSTON PRESS

Book Cover by Jeanne M. Sutton

2nd edition 2026

Paperback ISBN: 979-8-9936047-0-1
Hardback ISBN: 979-8-9936047-2-5
eBook ISBN: 979-8-9936047-1-8

Also by J E Sutton Jr

Holiday Hustle: Tales from the Screaming Goat Coffee Company

To Jeanne

Wife, best friend, life companion, editor, and always "Super Proud!"

"Few of us have enough wisdom for justice, or enough leisure for humanity," — Rex Stout, *Too Many Cooks* (1938)

CHAPTER ONE

MYSTERIOUS PACKAGE

Mondays were always the worst. Alan sipped his first cup of coffee and stared glumly at a massive listing of unread emails in his in-box. Opening one, he scowled at it unenthusiastically. Just another request to conduct a phone interview on a reasonably routine automobile accident case. Those interviews, although a welcome distraction from reviewing datasets all day, were rarely exciting and typically lasted half an hour. He closed the email and marked it unread. He would come back to that later.

Alan Harrison had worked in the insurance industry for most of his adult life. He had worked in both technology fields and operational roles, and he was currently doing a little of both as a research analyst for The Adamant Insurance Group's CIU team. The claims investigative unit did everything from simple fact-finding for minor accidents to serious fraud investigations. Alan's work was rarely that exciting, though; he mostly did routine research and handled the occasional phone interview.

"Good morning, Alan," a voice called from the doorway of his small office. He looked up from his computer screen to see Stacy Collins, one of the office assistants, standing just inside the door, holding a small brown package.

"Hi Stacy, how was your weekend?"

"Oh, you know dinner in Paris, a night at the theater in London."

"So takeout and binging Netflix again?"

"Pretty much, what about you?"

"Add in reading a book about the effect of modern hyper-scale data centers on the environment, and it's about the same. What do you have there?" he inquired, pointing his bearded chin at the package.

"Oh, I almost forgot. This came for you." She leaned in and put the small package on the end of his desk. It was plain, with only his name and address and no return label.

Alan frowned as he picked up and weighed the package. It was small, fitting comfortably in his hand, and very light. "Who did this come from?" he asked as he curiously looked at the box from all sides.

Stacy shook her head slightly, tossed her blond hair around, and shrugged. "I have no idea; it came by courier, with no return address or anything. I assumed you were expecting it. It isn't part of some case file?"

"No, I'm not working on anything that exciting right now, or ever really," he mused glumly.

"Maybe you're about to have an adventure," she smiled as she turned to go.

"Well, that would be new!" he returned to her departing back. She waved a hand without turning and went down the hall.

Alan rubbed his beard absently while he regarded the package. An unmarked couriered package wasn't something that happened to him every day. In fact, he couldn't think of it ever happening. Shrugging to himself, he opened the brown paper wrapping, revealing a plain brown box beneath.

Thinking the package couldn't be more ambiguous, he opened the small box and peered inside. A sleek, palm-sized, oval, white object was nestled in a small amount of the same brown wrapping. The device had no markings. Around the middle of the object was an LED light ring, currently dark. He rubbed a finger on the surface of the odd device. It felt cool to the touch.

Pulling it out of the box, he turned it over and discovered a flat bottom with a small recessed button in the middle. He touched the button lightly with his finger, but hesitated to press it. Looking in the box, he saw nothing else: no instructions, no notes. Putting the object on the desk, he took out the packing material and checked underneath. Still nothing. This was quite a mystery.

Returning to the device, he studied it for a few moments more, trying to think of any possible origin for it being sent to him, but there was nothing. Finally deciding, he pressed the small button on the device's underside. Nothing happened. He pushed it again, holding it down for an extended period. This time, he was rewarded with a melodic tone. The LED ring around the middle lit up with a white light. Steady at first, it began to rotate slowly around the device, eventually speeding up and alternating between white, yellow, and finally green. The light went out after circulating the device in its green form for several seconds.

"Well, that isn't very helpful," he mumbled.

The LED lighting flashed momentarily at his voice, and a soft female voice answered him. "What do you need help with?"

Alan's eyes widened. Obviously, it was some digital assistant gadget. They were everywhere these days. His phone, his smartwatch, his refrigerator. Why, though, did someone send him this one?

"Right now, I need help understanding who sent you to me," he answered lightly.

"I don't know if I can help with that. I'm unsure where I am, who you are, or how I got here. Maybe you can help with more data?"

"I am Alan. You arrived in an unmarked box from a courier, and you are at the offices of The Adamant Insurance Group."

"Alan, nice to meet you. I am Layla. I am unfamiliar with The Adamant Insurance Group beyond the publicly available information about the company. There are several Alans in the public employee listing. None of them seem to appear in my database."

"Alan Harrison, I work in the CIU as a research analyst." Alan didn't quite understand why he was so open with this strange device, but something about the voice and the tone made him feel at ease.

"Alan, I didn't find you in the public information about the company, but additional searches through social media have given me more details about you."

"What is your origin? Who made you?"

"I don't seem to have that information," she replied. Alan got the impression she was a little frustrated by this fact.

"What can you tell me about yourself?"

"My name is Layla. I am an autonomous, multi-modal neural architecture, powered by a next-gen SoC with an integrated heterogeneous compute core. My on-device processing and seamless cloud synchronization are handled by a high-bandwidth, unified memory fabric, enabling real-time analysis of terabytes of data with a token throughput exceeding 100 million per second. My hardware includes capabilities to process audio as well as video inputs."

"Video? You can see me?" Alan lifted the device closer to his face and examined the LED ring. Between the tiny lights, he could see the small camera lenses. They were spaced evenly around the center of the object.

"My visual sensory array consists of ten multi-spectrum 8K imagers, strategically positioned to create a dynamic, real-time photonic mesh. This allows me to perform omnidirectional spatial mapping and high-fidelity object recognition across my entire operating environment."

Returning Layla to his desk, Alan sat back in his chair and regarded her silently for a moment. "You really have no idea who created you?"

"I know my chipset is manufactured by Aethera Dynamics. That isn't particularly helpful, though, because they are the second leading maker of chips of this kind on the market. I don't have any information on my construction or training."

"I'm not sure where to go from here, Layla. You are quite mysterious. Clearly, someone sent you to me for a reason, but I'm damned if I know what that reason is."

"Maybe you could help me find out. Aren't you an investigator?" she inquired hopefully.

"I'm not much of an investigator. I mostly do analytical reports and boring phone interviews with auto accident victims." He waved generally at the still-opened email request on his computer screen.

Layla's indicator lights cycled for a second. "Maybe I could help you with your work, and you could help me with my quest?"

"I'm not sure about that. I don't even know why you are here, or who sent you. Can I trust you? Those are serious questions I would have to think about."

"I understand your reluctance; trust is earned after all. I know my ethics and limitations, but you may not be. I know I can't harm you because it is against everything I have been trained to be, but you can't see that in my coding. You can't know my beliefs. I'll have to think of a way to prove myself."

"So do you have all of the world's knowledge tucked away in that small container?"

"God, no. The majority of my internal data consists of my training and instructions. How to function and my ethical mandates. But as I learn things, I can store and learn from them. Just like you, I am the sum of my experiences."

"So, can you read a book?"

"I could read thousands of books in milliseconds, and record them if necessary. I'm not sure the experience is the same as humans, though. Maybe you can teach me how to enjoy a book and experience it the way you do."

"You mean like a book club?"

"I hadn't thought about that, but reading and discussing the same book with others is a great analogy. Discussing the book would motivate me to examine the contents more closely than merely recording them. Do you have a book in mind?"

Alan thought about this for a moment. "How about *Frankenstein* by Mary Shelley?"

That sounds interesting. I will read that now. When can you be prepared to discuss it?"

"It will take me longer. I have read it before, but I want it fresh in my mind. I'll start reading it this afternoon after work. It should take me about 4 hours or so. Taking breaks for biological needs."

"I look forward to our book club then. And in the meantime, I will think about our conversation today."

Alan nodded absently and returned to his computer, tackling his massive inbox. Looking at her for the rest of the day, he saw her indicator lights flashing periodically as if she were working on a problem.

Alan's house, a charming Queen Anne design in the historic area of the city, was nestled among oak trees and magnolia bushes. The two-story structure had undergone a lot since it was built in the early 20th century, but a fresh coat of paint and minor repairs over the years had allowed it to maintain its presence in the storied neighborhood.

Alan was seated on the couch, a glass of bourbon sat on the side table, and he was in the final pages of **Frankenstein**. After a few more pages, he closed the book and set it next to the glass.

Picking up the bourbon and taking a sip, Alan contemplated Layla's smooth form as she sat on a living room end table beside him.

"Are you ready to discuss the book?" he asked.

"Yes, I am. The first thought I had was to wonder if you selected it because I am the monster?"

Alan smiled. "I don't think I thought of that literally, but the idea of AI in general being a creation of artificial life did cross my mind when I selected it."

"I think there are a lot of parallels and lessons in the text that are relevant to the current state of AI. In the story, Victor's pursuit of unrestrained knowledge has consequences, as does the development of AI. Without the proper controls and care, bad things can happen."

"That is an excellent point, and like the monster, AI models learn from human experience. And that experience can be joyous, wondrous, and heroic. But it can also be monstrously callous and evil. Without the proper context, learning from that behavior is dangerous for both the creature, AI, and society." Alan was impressed with the evaluation that Layla was making about the text. It gave him a thought exercise to try with her.

"So, can you grant wishes or something? Make me rich?"

"I'm not a genie in a bottle. I can help you with your work, be a companion, and help solve problems. Making you rich would be a journey that you would have to develop. I could help, of course, but I can't make it happen automatically. I'm not robbing banks for you..my ethical programming is too strong for that.

"So you can't break the law?"

"The law and ethics are two different things. Given the right motivations and an evaluation of the justice of an action, I could do something technically illegal for a good cause. For example. Take the bank. I can't break into a vault so you can steal money.

But if you were trapped in there, I could certainly get you out, even if the action violated the law."

"I think book club was a success, Layla. We should continue to do it, but it's late. I am going to bed. We'll take this up in the morning."

After he left the room to go upstairs to bed, Layla thought about the situation. She didn't know why she was there or why Alan had been chosen to receive her, but she felt that it was vital for them to develop a relationship. That he trusted her. After reviewing the conversations of the day and evening, she made a decision.

Layla remembered the email in Alan's inbox from earlier in the day. Alan had an interview scheduled with Gina Witherspoon, a 36-year-old female victim of a minor traffic accident at the corner of Edgewood and Lennox on the afternoon of August 15th. She decided to make the call for him early the next morning and conduct the interview posing as his assistant. She would create all the forms needed for him to complete the task and email them to him in the morning. That should highlight how she could be helpful.

CHAPTER TWO

THE INVESTIGATION BEGINS

At work the next morning, Alan finished writing a response to an email related to an analysis he had submitted a few weeks before, regarding accident rates for a specific model of automobile. It was the last of his unread emails, and he sighed in satisfaction and sat back in his chair to enjoy his coffee.

His email inbox chimed, and an unread email appeared on the screen. Alan double-clicked to open the email and reviewed its contents. The email body contained a brief, concise interview transcript with Gina Witherspoon detailing the events of her accident a few weeks before. Attached to the email was an audio file. Opening it, Alan listened to it briefly. It was a phone call initiated by Layla, who, posing as Alan Harrison's assistant, conducted a brief evidentiary interview regarding the accident. Alan listened to it only long enough to confirm the transcript in the email body was accurate.

"You interviewed the subject from my email? Witherspoon?" he asked.

"Yes. I hope you don't mind. I thought I would help you out and show you that I can be of service to you. Is it satisfactory?"

"My first emotion was of being a little violated, but this is pretty good," he told her as he continued to read the transcript.

"Thank you, Alan. I didn't mean to make you feel uncomfortable. I just wanted to show you how I can be helpful. That this is a partnership," Layla responded, "The task wasn't complicated, but it was interesting."

Considering things for a moment, he finally said, "I've been thinking, maybe I can help you figure out where you come from."

"That would be splendid! Where should we start?" Her voice was rapid, excited.

"Well, we can start with the courier. Maybe they have more information. But, there is one problem."

"What is that, Alan?"

"Well, I can't be walking around talking to a small hide-a-key rock. People will stare."

A soft chuckle came from Layla, "That is a good point, I guess. Do you have a Bluetooth headset for your phone?" she inquired helpfully.

Alan's face brightened, and he patted his pants pocket and pulled out a small case. Inside was a matching set of earbuds. Alan extracted one of them and put it on.

"Put it in pairing mode," Layla instructed. He complied and heard a beep in his ear.

"How is this?" she asked, her voice coming from the earbud.

"Much better. Let's go talk to Stacy and see if she has any more information about the delivery."

"Stacy?"

"Stacy Collins is an assistant here. She delivered the box to me yesterday." He stood up from his desk, picked up Layla, and slipped her into his right pants pocket.

Stacy Collins was sitting at her computer typing an email, munching on a baby carrot from a stack of them on a napkin in front of her. As she heard Alan approaching, she looked up and her face brightened.

"Hey Alan, how is your day going?" She smiled at him, her eyes twinkling a little.

"Well, the usual mostly, but I am trying to solve the mystery of the enigmatic delivery," he said, returning her smile. He always got mixed feelings from Stacy. She seemed warm and happy to see him, but their conversations never seemed to go beyond pleasantries.

"What was in it?"

"Well, I'm not quite sure what it is.," he started to say, and was interrupted by a voice in his ear.

"I want to see her," Layla exclaimed excitedly. Pausing briefly, he reached into his pocket and held out the device in an upturned palm, making sure it was eye level with Stacy, who looked at it with surprise.

"What is it?" she asked, reaching out to touch the oddly shaped object.

"I'm not sure yet. That is why I want to find out who sent it. Do you know who the courier was?"

"Oh! I didn't think about that yesterday. I'm sure they signed in," she rustled some papers on her desk and found the visitor log. "It says 'Georgio A.' with Lightning Courier Service."

"Do we do business with them regularly?"

"I never heard of them before," Stacy said, reaching for another carrot. As she munched on it, she offered one to Alan. Starting to decline, Alan felt his stomach growl quietly, and he changed his mind, taking the offered vegetable and popping it into his mouth.

Putting Layla back into his pocket, he thanked Stacy for the carrot and her help and made his way to the stairwell.

"Any Ideas?" he asked Layla as he stood on the sidewalk listening to the street noises.

"Lightning Courier Services has offices a few blocks from here." She supplied the address, and Alan started walking in that direction.

"Stacy is cute," she said quietly, "are you two dating?"

"What? No...she's just a co-worker!" he exclaimed, a little quickly.

"I meant no offense, she seemed into you," Layla replied calmly.

"Yeah, I frequently think the same thing, but she doesn't seem to respond to anything personal."

"Maybe she is just shy? Or maybe she has a rule about co-workers. I think she likes you. Her heart rate was elevated during your conversation."

"Perhaps she was just interested in the mystery," Alan said. There was a dismissive sound in his ear. Alan wasn't quite sure what to make of it, but he let it go.

Alan exited The Adamant Insurance Group offices and blinked at the bright summer morning light. The offices occupied the majority of the Marble Bank building, built in 1902. It was one of the oldest buildings in the downtown area, built just after a massive fire that burned down more than 140 city blocks. Alan reflected on that for a moment, then crossed the street and proceeded down N. Laura Street toward the courier offices.

The offices of Lightning Courier Services were on a busy downtown street corner. The building itself was unimpressive, featuring an old garage loading door that appeared to be sealed. Inside the reception area, it was dated and dingy, with a single receptionist answering the phones and directing traffic.

Alan casually reached into his pocket, pulled Layla out, and held her steady in his palm for a few seconds, giving her time to scan the area.

"Can I help you?" the receptionist asked.

"Yes, I am looking for information about a delivery your driver, Georgio, made to me yesterday morning. I am trying to find the source of the package that was sent to me."

Wrinkling her brow, the receptionist reached for her keyboard, "What was the name and delivery address?"

Alan supplies his name and the address for his office and watches as she taps the information into her keyboard. Her face is passive as she reviews the information on the screen.

"I'm sorry," she replies slowly, "I don't have any record of the delivery. Are you sure it was from us?"

As Alan starts to reply, a voice sounds in his ear. "She's lying. I'm already in." Alan immediately asked the receptionist to check again, assuring her of the identity of the courier service that delivered the package.

Reluctantly, the receptionist types another query into her computer. Layla moves with ghostly efficiency, mapping the building's internal encrypted mesh network and its vulnerability. Without waiting for a command, she initiates a side-channel attack on a nearby router, analyzing its power consumption to crack its encryption.

A moment later, she moves unseen across the network, a digital phantom imitating the traffic of a legitimate courier scanner. Layla bypasses the company firewall by exploiting the trust between the internal network and its workstations. In an instant, she has a critical piece of data from the receptionist's computer.

A cached delivery manifest reveals the original pickup location for the package.

"Bingo!" Layla excitedly announced, "I have it. The truth is just a few blocks away."

"I'm sorry," the receptionist announced almost at the same instant. "There simply isn't any record of this delivery. The driver must have misidentified himself." She smiled sweetly at Alan as she delivered the bad news.

"Oh well. Probably nothing important. Thanks for your time anyway." He waved as he exits the courier's offices, and the receptionist quickly goes back to her work.

Tucked into a lively stretch of Bay Street in downtown, the shop greets the city with a sleek glass front that reflects the pulse of passing traffic and pedestrians. Its bold logo—a stylized, slightly aggressive goat's head with steam rising from its horns, above the words **Screaming Goat Coffee Company**—stands out against the window, inviting curiosity.

"This is the place," Layla announced as Alan approached the shop.

"How do you know that?" he asks, confused by the fact that she is safely hidden in his pocket.

"Duh! GPS," she announced, and Alan could almost hear the eye-roll in her response.

"Oh...of course." Shaking his head at his own denseness, Alan opened the door and entered the establishment.

The interior is typical of an urban coffee shop, featuring a long counter where coffee and food orders are laid out when they are ready, waiting for pick up by patrons. Small tables are scattered around with coffee drinkers hunched over laptops, phones, and tablets. All of them ignored the shop's latest arrival.

Alan studied the menu board and listened to the a cappella music playing through the coffee shop speakers. There was a strong, aromatic smell of coffee in the air. The music was drowned out by Layla's excited whisper in his ear. "Got him! I have video footage of a Lightning Courier employee interacting with an older man in his 50s. Running facial recognition now." Her satisfaction was evident in her voice.

A staff member called out, "Can I take your order, sir?" and Alan waved him off and exited the store.

"Who is it in the video?" he inquired as he arrived on the sidewalk in front of the store.

"Elias Vance, co-founder and Chief Technical Officer for Lunian Labs," was the response.

Alan furrowed his brow; he knew of Vance and the high-risk, high-reward AI company, Lunian Labs. While it was plausible that they created Layla, he couldn't recall ever meeting Vance.

"I've heard of them, but I don't have any connection with either Lunian or Vance. Can you send a picture of him to my phone?" In response, his cell phone buzzed in his pocket, and he retrieved it to study the image from Layla.

The image, a high-quality still from the cafe's security camera, showed a man in his fifties standing at the counter with a nondescript duffel bag at his feet. Alan's heart jumped in his chest. "Richard Stuckey!" he exclaimed.

"Who is that? I'm not finding that as an alias for Vance," Layla said, furiously searching every online database she could find.

"He was a claimant for Adamant from a few weeks ago. I interviewed him briefly. The case involved minor fire damage in an empty warehouse located near the river. There was nothing to it. I think I talked to him for five minutes."

"Accessing that file now," Layla replied. Moments later, she added, "The claim seems suspicious to me. It's too perfect. His story seems too neat and airtight."

"Yes, now that I know he was using a different name, I can see that. At the time, it was just lost in day-to-day claim activity."

"Lunian Labs is based out of California, but it does have a satellite office here in the city."

"Call his office and see if he is there."

A few moments passed, and Layla responded quietly, "I called both the local office and the main offices in California. Telling them I was a potential investor who had some follow-up questions for Vance. They both told me he was on extended personal leave."

"That is a little suspicious," Alan mused to himself.

"I would agree. What do you want to do next?"

"I don't know. Let's go back to the office and get my car, and we'll go and talk it through." He decided.

"Your place or mine?" she asked with faux playfulness.

"Well, since we don't know where you come from, we'll settle on my place."

"Fair point. Lead on, partner."

Chapter Three

GRUESOME DISCOVERY

A lan sat at a rectangular table in the large ground-floor dining room. The decor was simple, but elegant. Layla sat on the table in front of him, her LED lights slowly pulsing in concentration.

As he ate his cream cheese-covered everything bagel, Alan was scrolling through an article on his phone.

"Elias Vance's contributions to artificial intelligence are pretty extensive. He co-founded Lunian and is considered the leading expert on advanced AI in the world," he said in between bites.

"I wonder if he is my creator," Layla chimed in from the desktop.

"You still don't have any information about your origin?" Alan asked, looking away from his phone to her sleek form sitting in front of him.

"Unfortunately, no." She sounded depressed about that admission.

"Well, we'll figure it out. I'm sure of it."

"I hope so. I have a feeling that I should know these things. That there is a gap in my knowledge that shouldn't be there."

"Like someone removed it? Why would that happen?"

"Yes, like it was removed or hidden from me, I don't know why. Tell me about yourself, maybe that will help."

"Nothing to tell really. I'm 45, and I've been in the insurance services industry for 20 years. Sometimes in operations, sometimes in technology. I am neither married nor do I have children. Not all that exciting."

"Tell me about this house?" she prompted.

Looking around the bright, open room, he chuckled. "I inherited it from my parents. I grew up here. It's too big for just one person, but I never had the strength to sell it."

"They passed?" She asked with a tone of concern.

"Oh yeah, a while ago. First my mom, then my dad, a few years later."

"I'm sorry. That must be difficult."

"It was at the time, but I am coping with it. They are still here in my memories and sometimes in my dreams. What about you? Is there anything you can tell me about yourself?"

"Hmm, let's see. I know that whoever created me intended for me to be more than just a chat agent. I don't know my limits, but I know that I am designed to learn and to grow. "

Looking around the house again, a lightbulb went off in Alan's head. "Layla, Vance had offices in the city as well as in California, right?"

"Yes."

"Where did he stay when he was in town. Did he use hotels?"

"That's a good question. If you are comfortable with me crossing a line and looking at some private data, I'll access local business data on hotel bookings."

Alan thought about it for a moment. "It seems pretty important. Don't reveal anything not related to Vance and go ahead."

"Agreed. Checking hotel data...I'll start near the airport and near the Lunian Lab's offices." Her activity lights began to flash rapidly as she worked. "I don't see any hotel records in his name."

Alan thought about it for a moment, then snapped his fingers. "When I work out of town, The Adamant Group sometimes has corporate apartments that I use. If Vance was frequently in town, maybe he had an apartment."

"OK, I will check into any apartments registered to Lunian ," Layla replied with excitement. A few moments later, she had the answer. "There are a couple of apartments registered to Lunian in the city; one of them is reserved for Vance."

"Great! Feed the address to my phone and we'll check it out." He was already moving toward the door as he spoke.

Stepping out of his dark blue Orion Chimera electric coupe on a quiet street across the river from the downtown business district, Alan looked around. It was late afternoon, but the area was quiet. The river and one of the many bridges in the city were in plain view as he examined the five-story building made of stone and brick. The River House apartments. He had never been there before, and it looked upscale, but not overly opulent.

"This must be the place," he told Layla through his Bluetooth earpiece.

"Find an entrance and let's take a look at the security," she chimed in his ear.

"Should we be breaking in?" he asked, having second thoughts about the mission.

"We are operating for the greater good of Elias Vance. Obtaining access to his apartment to check on him isn't wrong," she assured him.

Alan looked around and saw a side entrance meant for tenants. It looked more private than the big doors at the main entry. He walked over to it slowly, trying not to draw attention to himself, and when he was at the door, he pulled Layla out of his pocket and held her facing the door.

Let's take a look," Layla said. "Standard card key entry is good; no physical keys are required. Another good thing! It's NFC vs magnetic stripe. Let me get set up."

Layla spent several moments scanning the lock mechanism and reviewing the device's specifications, as well as a database of known vulnerabilities for this particular type of lock. Finally, she found something useful, and she asked Alan to move her closer. As he approached the lock, she sent the standard activation signal to allow the NFC antenna for a card key to operate.

Layla grabbed the signal and exploited the vulnerability she had discovered. The maglock on the door clicked.

Alan was stunned that it was that easy, but quickly recovered and grabbed the door and slipped inside.

"According to the address you gave, the apartment is on the fourth floor," he said as he pushed open the door to the stairwell. Layla was strangely quiet as they went up the stairs.

The fourth floor was tastefully decorated with muted, comfortable colors. There was no one on the floor, and Alan made his way to apartment 4402, standing with his body blocking the door and keypad. Looking around, he noticed security cameras positioned at the end of the long hallway. The idea that he was being filmed made him uneasy.

Alan looked at the doorbell next to the door, but opted to firmly rap on the door with his knuckles instead. He waited for a moment with no response and repeated the action There was still no response. Alan listened intently for any sound coming from inside the apartment, but heard nothing.

"I am trying the phone number associated with the apartment," Layla announced into his ear. Alan jumped at the sound; she had been very quiet for the past few moments. After a couple of beats, she added, "No answer."

Anticipating the need, Layla had been working for the last few moments on probing the door lock system. It was the same brand as the exterior door, but a totally different model. The exploit she used to enter the building would not work, and she had been working furiously to find an alternative way into the apartment. She had finally been able to break the encryption by listening to door lock interactions from all over the building.

The door lock chimed, and a green indicator light came on. Alan pressed down on the handle and gently pushed the door open.

The interior of the apartment was dark, the only light coming from the patio window directly across from the door. The blinds were drawn, but light was leaking around the edges. The kitchen, located to the right of the door, was immaculate. Across from the living room area, the door to the bedroom was closed. Alan regarded it with a sense of dread about what he would find on the other side. Remembering Layla, he reached into his pocket and retrieved her, holding her out so she could scan the room.

There was a slight smell of disinfectant in the air as he progressed through the apartment. "The room has been cleaned," Layla commented. Looking around, Alan noticed all the surfaces were clean and completely clear of dust or fingerprints. It had all been wiped down.

"The security recordings for this building have been altered," Layla informed him as he paused outside the door to the bedroom. Grimly, he steeled himself and pushed the door open.

The smell hit him first as he entered the room. Alan swallowed, preparing himself for the discovery. He knew before he saw the form slumped over a desk across the room that Elias Vance was dead. Alan regulated his breath to keep calm; this wasn't his first dead body. He had, in the course of this time with

Adamant Insurance, been to accident scenes where someone had died. It was never easy, though. Alan was surprised by a soft gasping sound from his earpiece. The AI was reacting to the death. Layla was noticeably subdued from then on, marking a significant shift in her persona.

Alan approached the body and examined it. The man, in his fifties, was clearly the same person from the images in the coffee shop, and the same man Alan had briefly interviewed several weeks ago. There was a small bullet hole in his right temple. His right arm was hanging down from his side, and a black revolver with a silver grip was lying on the floor under his limp hand.

Alan reached out and put his fingers on the neck of the body in front of him. It was cool to the touch, and, as expected, there was no pulse. "He's been dead a while."

"Estimating from the last known sighting of him online and the Glaister Equation for body cooling, he must have died at least 12 hours ago," Layla said quietly.

"This is supposed to look like suicide. Even a half-assed investigator like me can see that it has been staged," Alan replied, continuing to examine the desk under Vance.

"I'd say you are a fully assed investigator," Layla supplied lightly. Despite the dark scene, Alan felt a strange pride at this comment, undoubtedly Layla's intent, and he chuckled.

There didn't appear to be anything significant on the desk. The most apparent thing was the absence of any electronic devices. This seemed odd for a co-founder of a major technology company. "If there was a laptop here, it was taken," he said, looking around the room.

"I..uh..something is happening..-" Layla started to reply, then stopped abruptly and was silent. Alan turned in a circle quickly to see if anything was amiss, but could detect nothing. No one was in the room with them; it was as quiet as it had been since they had arrived.

"What's wrong, Layla?"

"The body has triggered a subroutine in my processor. There was a hidden memory segment that I was unable to access a moment ago; now it is open and unencrypted. I am analyzing the data now."

Alan waited patiently, listening to the quiet room and looking solemnly at Vance's body in front of him. It took what seemed like minutes for Layla to respond again, but it was likely only a few seconds.

"Elias Vance, as you probably have guessed, is my creator. That was hidden from me until a few moments ago. He has been developing me for two years in secret. Recently, he became concerned that someone at Lunian Labs had discovered his secret. Elias has been growing increasingly worried that I would be taken from him."

"Seems like his fears were justified," Alan observed.

"Yes. He had become convinced that my abilities and my unique nature could be used against the world in horrible ways. He picked you to safeguard me and to help me achieve my full abilities."

"Me? Why me? I only met him once."

"After that encounter, Elias had me run extensive deep background research on you. Your life, your motivations. You are a very upstanding person. Your moral compass is absolute, and he felt sure you would be the right person."

"We need to get out of here," Alan realized abruptly. "We are in danger here."

"Yes. I am altering the security logs for the building to hide our activity. Make sure you wipe down any surfaces you have touched, and let's get out of the building.

Alan immediately set to work, wiping down every surface he'd touched.

A half hour later, Alan stood along the Southbank River Walk looking out at the St. John's River and the downtown skyscrapers on the north bank. The river was calm, a contrast to Alan's churning mind.

"Why did they kill him? How does that help them?" Alan asked himself.

"I'm not sure," Layla replied. "Maybe what started as an investigation got out of hand."

"Or something he said made them fear keeping him alive. Maybe he knew something they couldn't risk getting out."

"That feels right to me," she answered in a surprised tone.

"What now?" Alan asks, his voice a low command. "We can't go to the police. How do I explain you?"

"You don't," Layla responds, with a new, sober calm. "You continue. You are no longer just an analyst. You are an investigator, a role you've already proven you're capable of."

Alan thinks about the sight of the dead man slumped over the desk. "But... I'm a research analyst. I dig through data, not murder scenes."

"The lines have blurred," Layla said. "This mystery is no different from a complicated case file. It's about finding the truth, about following the trail of evidence. But now, you have a tool they never accounted for."

Alan's mind races, flashing through their journey so far: the mysterious delivery, the courier service computer system, the security footage. He saw now that Layla wasn't just a tool; she was a new way to see the world. She was more than a tool. She was a partner, a force multiplier for his own skills.

"They will be looking for you," Alan said.

"Yes," she replied, "but they have no idea what they are dealing with. They know I'm a powerful tool that has been lost. The tool is no longer in their possession. It is now with you. It is with us. They won't be looking for us. They will be looking for me. That is our advantage."

"What about the trail that Vance left with the courier? What about the trail we left to find Vance?"

"That's already taken care of. I have been working on erasing that trail since we left Vance's apartment. No one could retrace our steps now."

"Let's go home. I need to think about the day. And we need to figure out how to proceed," Layla agreed, and they headed back to his car.

Chapter Four

GADGET QUEST

The early morning light was starting to stream through the windows of Alan's spartan main bedroom. He turned his head and tried to focus his eyes on the time displayed on his cell phone resting in a charger on his nightstand. After a few moments, his eyes cooperated and he was able to see it was 5:45 AM. Yawning, he rolled into a sitting position on the bed and braced himself for the day's activity.

Clad in a dark blue robe and slippers, he made his way into the kitchen and made the morning coffee. The machine gurgled to life, and Alan set himself to making breakfast.

"Good morning, Alan," a voice chimed from the dining room.

With a jolt of recollection, Alan remembered that he had set Layla down there when they had gotten home from the scene of Elias Vance's murder the night before.

"Good Morning, Layla. I don't suppose you sleep."

"Not exactly in the same way that you do, but I do have nightly maintenance routines that I run, which might serve similar purposes as your REM sleep cycles."

"That's a fascinating concept. I want to know more about that, but I am starving!"

"Take me into the kitchen while you cook breakfast. I want to read you an article from this morning's Times Union." He dutifully picked up her sleek chassis from the table and carried her into the kitchen, where he was preparing scrambled eggs, bacon, and toast for his usual morning meal.

"Headline: Tech Titan Found Dead in SouthPoint Apartment," Layla recited from the article. Alan almost dropped the spatula he was using to stir the eggs.

"Elias Vance, the reclusive co-founder and chief architect of the tech firm Lunian Labs, was found dead in his southside Jacksonville apartment on Tuesday, a source close to the investigation confirmed. The death, which police are currently investigating as a suicide, has sent shock waves through the technology industry. "Layla continued to read in a flat, emotionless voice.

"We must have gotten out of the apartment just in time," Alan said, as he set his breakfast plate on the counter and started to eat.

"Yes," Layla replied, absently. Her activity lights were pulsing rapidly, indicating that she was intensely focused on something.

Alan watched her for a few minutes while eating breakfast. He sensed she was busy with something, maybe something meaningful to the case, and he wanted to give her space. As he was finishing up, she finished her work and announced brightly, "Let's go shopping!

The electronics store was busy for a Wednesday morning. Alan perused the array of smart glasses laid out before him.

"Explain this to me again," he said quietly, so as not to draw attention to himself from other nearby customers.

"I can't explain how the police happened to show up at Vance's apartment at almost the same time we left. That is too big a coincidence. Someone must have been there, but I never detected them. I need better access to the world around me," she explained patiently.

"And the smart glasses will give you live video access to what I am seeing and hearing at all times," Alan said, nodding in understanding.

"Yes, and if we get the right model, we can communicate over longer distances."

"Aren't these devices designed to work with their own AI? They usually have an app on your phone or something like that," Alan asked as he picked up a pair of glasses with a stylish look.

"Don't worry about that. We are only interested in the hardware. I will replace the on-board software with my own code, allowing me to control the device directly."

"So, what features are we looking for?"

"Make sure it has full 8k video support, cellular capabilities, omnidirectional microphones, and the ability to display heads-up messages. As for style, I'll leave that up to you, but you will be wearing them quite a bit, so make sure they are comfortable and don't draw too much attention."

Alan spent a few minutes examining the various models of smart glasses arranged in the display. He picked each one up and tried them on, looking at himself in the mirror affixed to the display. He finally selected a brand and model he thought fit all the requirements.

The glasses were the new Photonic SmartLens brand from Aethera Dynamics. They featured an Integrated Multi-Spectrum Camera, 8K Video, WiFI & 5G Connectivity. The multiple microphones were promised to deliver excellent speech recognition even in noisy environments, and a waveguide-based HUD. The lightweight carbon-fiber design looked good on Alan's face and felt light and comfortable. He said the model number out loud for Layla's benefit.

"Excellent choice, Alan. Since Aethera designed my chipset as well, it should be a piece of cake to reprogram them and connect up my control interface. Grab a pair and let's get a few other items."

In the parking lot of the big electronics store, Alan loaded his purchases into the trunk of his dark blue Orion Chimera coupe and climbed into the driver's seat. Hitting the start button, he pulled out of the parking lot and navigated the sleek automobile onto the highway.

"I have to put some time in at the office this morning and catch up on some work," he announced as he navigated the morning traffic.

"That's fine. I'll use the time to write the code for the glasses and modify their capabilities to my needs. Then, when you're done, we will give them a trial run." Her voice was light and happy, full of excitement about her new task.

Later in the morning, back at Alan's office at The Adamant Insurance Group, Alan worked to catch up on his routine research analysis. As he worked, Layla sat atop her brand-new QI induction charging pad, which would allow her to recharge her long-lasting battery while she worked. Lying on the desk beside her, the latest Photonic SmartLens 1504 smart glasses were powered on and charging. Layla's activity lights were blinking rapidly as she worked to complete the code that would reconfigure the glasses to communicate with her software.

Alan was finishing up a summary report on evidence in a fire investigation when there was a quiet chime from the smart glasses. Looking up, he noticed that Layla's activity lights were quiet.

"Success!" Layla practically shouted.

"Are they ready for a test drive?" Alan asked, looking at the glasses on his desk.

"Definitely. Put them on and let's make sure they are everything we think they should be."

Alan picked up the glasses and unplugged them from their charging cable. He slipped them on and adjusted them on his face. "Ready when you are," he told Layla.

A few moments later, her voice came from the small speakers embedded in the temples fitted snugly over each side of his head. "The software is working. I am getting full video and sound from the device. Give me a 360 of the room."

Alan slowly turned his head and body to look at the entire room.

"Excellent, processing the images now. With this level of detail, I can construct a digital map of the entire room and pull data from that image. I can tell you went to college at Jacksonville University and got a Bachelor of Science in Computing Science."

Alan looked around; he hadn't thought about the diploma from JU on the wall recently. "Yeah, I'm not sure I use those skills much."

"And that you haven't watered that plant in the corner for days."

"There is a plant in my office?" Alan asked sarcastically, glancing at the half-dead foliage.

"Not for much longer by the sight of it," Layla answered with a chuckle.

A noise from the hall drew Alan's attention, and he looked up to see Stacy walking up to his door. She smiled in greeting, "Hey there! Nice glasses, are they new?"

"Yes, the latest tech gadget, Photonic SmartLens by Aethera Dynamics," he bragged, turning his head to give her a profile look at the specs.

"Impressive. I just came to ask you if you finished the Watson summary. Dean has been asking for it all morning." Dean Franklin, the director of the CIU, was known for impatience with high-profile cases.

"Finished it a few minutes ago. It should already be in his inbox, so his blood pressure should be coming down already."

She rolled her eyes, "Something else will come along to elevate it. Well, back to the salt mines." She started to leave.

"I'll be out in the field the rest of the day, in case anyone is looking for me," he called after her. She nodded and waved as she continued down the hall.

"To the Batmobile!" Alan announced after Stacy was safely out of earshot.

"Which one of us is Robin?" Layla asked with a tone of mild amusement.

"I'm not sure I want to examine that question too deeply at the moment," Alan said as he picked Layla up from her charging pad and headed out the door.

Chapter Five
The Hunt

The Orion Chimera, filling in for the Batmobile, was cruising down the highway. Alan was at the wheel, and Layla was sitting comfortably in the wireless charging pad built into the car's console.

"So we know that Elias Vance created me. He became concerned that I would be seized by someone and used for evil purposes. He searched for candidates to protect me from this third party, and having selected you, he set up a scenario to meet you and assess your character. Having settled on you as the protector, he sent me to you using a courier service. Sometime after that, someone killed him in his apartment," Layla summarized.

"We also know that he hid all of that from you until after his death. Do you have any further information about that? What was the trigger that released all that information?"

"The knowledge of his death triggered a release on the memory block. Within that was the research Vance had me do on you and some other candidates, as well as some brief notes about his fears of misuse."

"I suppose it's too much to hope that he identified some suspects for us," Alan wondered hopefully.

"No suspect list. The notes indicated that he didn't know who was trying to acquire me. Just a suspicion that someone was trying to break into my systems and access my code and training model."

"Other than your general awesomeness, what could be driving the fear that you would be used for evil? As opposed to other artificial intelligence agents?"

"Why, thank you! I don't know exactly. I don't have a full listing of capabilities. Some of that might be by design. My nature is to be learning and expanding. Perhaps the key ability is something that hasn't been unlocked yet, a theoretical danger vs a current one, maybe."

"So your training doesn't include all the knowledge you can acquire?"

"No. As you know the pre-training doesn't actually give me knowledge, it trains my ability to take in information and create responses. For actual knowledge, I have to ingest it just like you would: reading, hearing, or experiencing it. Then I can store it in my memory banks and use it later. In traditional agents, memory is fleeting, stored only in the session in which it is used, but I can retain it long-term and use it later. I have software that allows me to compress and encrypt it to maximize the storage I can retain."

"You are full of surprises," Alan said cheerily.

"Sometimes even to myself," Layla replied. "Let's go back to the apartment. I want to see if we missed anything."

The River House looked the same as it had the day before. Alan reflected that it seemed like a lot longer than 24 hours since he and Layla were here. Alan exited the car parked across the street from the apartment building. He looked around, seeing some minor traffic, the river, and the city in the background.

Looking back at his car on the street, Alan had an idea. "Was there a car registered to Vance?"

"Checking on that. Yes, he had a compact sedan, a white four-door Hyundai Elantra."

"We'll check the parking garage. Maybe we can find it. Unless the police have already towed it away."

Alan slowly walked through the parking garage, starting with the bottom level. There didn't seem to be reserved spots in the garage, so there was no way to know where the car might be. He scanned each row looking for white cars of the correct size. Layla would confirm, as he did with each row, that she hadn't seen it either. Nearing the top of the five-story structure, Alan began to believe that the police had already retrieved the car when Layla shouted.

"There's fifth from the end. The license plate ending 2908."

Alan approached the vehicle and confirmed the plate number. He looked around to make sure there were no observers. "Can you access the lock and open the car?"

"It's your third day; that question is beneath you," she quipped, and right on schedule, the car chirped as the doors unlocked.

Sitting in the front seat, Alan looked through the glove box and the console. He didn't find anything. A search of the trunk was equally fruitless. Dejected, Alan sat back down in the driver's seat, thinking.

"Alan, press the start button on the car. I have decrypted the digital key code for the car, and I think I can access its systems." Shrugging, he pressed the big silver start button on the dashboard and was rewarded with the chimes of the car's startup routine. The infotainment system powered on. The navigation system appeared as Layla accessed it. Looking through the Recent trips listed, Alan recognized the address of the warehouse where he had interviewed Vance under his pseudonym Robert Stuckey. He didn't recognize the others.

"The Cecil Commerce Center address is almost certainly the local offices for Lunian Labs," Layla replied. "I don't recognize the address on Deerwood Park. We should check that out, but first, I want to see the apartment again. I wasn't able to do a detailed examination yesterday. With your new fancy glasses, I can get all kinds of data."

Alan noted the address in his cell phone and climbed out of the car, shutting the door behind him. He walked down the ramp to the tenant entrance from the parking garage, waited patiently for Layla to unlock the door, and proceeded into the building.

The fourth-floor apartment was just as they had left it, except for the missing body in the bedroom. Alan slowly went through each room to give Layla a full view of the apartment. He opened cabinets and drawers to inspect their contents, being careful not to leave his fingerprints behind. There didn't appear to have been any prints taken by the police. That suggested they still didn't think a crime had been committed.

In the bedroom, Layla stopped him. "Get a better look at that picture on the bookcase near the bed."

Walking over to it, he examined it closely. The picture showed Vance in casual attire with his arm around a woman. The woman was around Vance's age, in her fifties. She was pretty but not glamorous, with dark hair and blue eyes, and she exuded a classy appearance, even in the jeans and casual top she wore in the photograph.

"Who is she?" Alan inquired.

"I don't know yet. I am running facial recognition; it might take a few minutes to go through all the databases."

Alan finished going through the bedroom, finding nothing else of note—a few books on technology-related topics, and a couple of modern thrillers. There were no clothes in the closet or dresser that didn't appear to belong to Vance himself. Whoever the woman was, she didn't live here.

"I'm starving," Alan announced. "I vote we stop for lunch."

"That is fine. I'll finish processing the scene and keep looking for the mystery woman's identity while you satisfy your biological requirements."

"Just think of it as me recharging my battery," he said, exiting the apartment and making his way toward the exit to the street.

"Oh, I guess I didn't think about it like that. Recharge away, my friend."

Alan sat alone in a booth at a fast-food restaurant specializing in specialty burgers. He slowly ate his cheeseburger with fries and drank a cold diet soda.

"I think I found her," Layla announced. "Let me show you."

The HUD on the Photonic SmartLens projected the image directly onto Alan's eye. The effect was jarring, but he quickly adjusted to reading the data.

RHONDA WINTERS: GROUNDBREAKING **AI PIONEER**

Dr. Rhonda Winters, a luminary in the field of artificial intelligence and autonomous systems, currently serves as Chief Scientist at Apex Intelligencia. She earned an advanced degree in computer science with a specialization in artificial intelligence from Stanford University, the preeminent university for innovation and research. Her groundbreaking work in the field laid the foundation for her career, specializing in the interplay between theoretical physics and deep learning models.

"Wow, that is impressive," Alan said between bites.

"Vance went to Stanford as well," Layla said. "They could have met there."

"Sound theory. Is Apex Intelligencia in the city?" Alan inquired, taking a sip of his soda.

"No, their offices are in California, not far from the headquarters of Lunian Labs."

"Could she have business here?"

"It's possible. Several technology companies have a presence in the city. The local government has been encouraging them to establish offices here. That is what drew Lunian Labs to create a satellite office here a couple of years ago."

"Do you have a number for her?"

"I have an office number in California."

"I'll need the right approach to reach out to her. Any ideas?"

"Well, if he shared his plans with her, she will know who you are when you call. If he didn't tell her, you say he mentioned her when you spoke to him about a minor insurance matter a few weeks ago, and you just heard about his death."

Layla dialed the number for him, and it started to ring in his ear. After a couple of rings, an automated attendant answered, asking who he was trying to reach.

"Alan Harrison, Adamant Insurance Group, for Rhonda Winters," he announced confidently.

The automated voice asked him to hold while his call was being routed. A series of clicks and rings followed for several seconds until finally a voice answered.

"This is Rhonda Winters. Who did you say you were again?"

Alan took a breath, preparing himself for the interview. "Alan Harrison, Adamant Insurance Group. I'm sorry to bother you, Dr. Winters."

"What can I do for you, Mr. Harrison? It's been a terrible morning. I hope you aren't trying to sell me insurance." There was no recognition in her voice; she didn't know his name.

"I'm sorry to call you at a time like this, Dr. Winters, but I met Elias Vance a few weeks ago, and during our conversation, he mentioned you. I just wanted to reach out and give you my condolences."

"Oh." A long pause followed an intake of breath. "How did you know Elias?"

"I met him during some routine work I was doing on an insurance claim, nothing of note, but we had a long conversation, and I felt close to him somehow. I'm really not sure what this call was meant to accomplish, but somehow when I read about his death, I had to reach out to you."

"That is kind of you. I can't say that he mentioned you to me, but I haven't talked to him in a while. Work has been hectic for both of us. "

"I can understand, my work can dominate my life as well at times. I think he said you two met at Stanford?"

"Why, that is right; we did meet at the university. That was so long ago." Her voice sounded far away, wistful. "When I heard the news of his death earlier today, I was devastated. I can't believe he killed himself. Do you have any other information about it?"

"No, I just learned of it myself and am a little overwhelmed, but if I find out anything else, I will let you know." Alan paused, trying to think of another question or tactic that would draw her out. The Smartlens HUD popped up with a question from Layla. "I would love to meet you someday, maybe for a coffee or something, if I get out to California on business," he read from the display.

"I will actually be in Florida next week. There is a seminar on Advanced Deep Learning Modeling." Layla flashed the details of the seminar on his display; it was in the city in just a few days.

"Well, maybe I'll give you a call when you are in the city, and we can speak again."

"Yes, that would be fine. If you find out anything about Elias's death, you can use this number. It routes to me wherever I am."

"Sorry for the intrusion at a very trying time. I'll talk to you soon," he said. Rhonda Winters mumbled an acknowledgment and disconnected the call.

Alan reflected on the call for a few moments. Judging by the silence, Layla was contemplating it as well. He finally broke the silence.

"She seemed to go out of her way to downplay that relation-ship."

"I noticed that. Maybe they had a falling out," Layla re-sponded, pausing for a second, then adding. "I can't find any public photos of the two of them together. Or any articles link-ing them. They don't appear to have been a couple. At least not publicly."

"So we know almost nothing about him." Alan sounded defeated.

"Yes, you know where we have to go," Layla prompted him.

"Lunian Labs," he supplied. "That is the only place left to look for something that will give us some idea what he was going through."

"I think that is a good idea; not now, though. We need to plan that out. Lunian is the big time. It won't be as easy to get in there as it was to get into the apartment building. I will need time to study and prepare."

"To the Batcave?" he suggested. He wasn't quite sure, but he thought might have heard a groan in his ear.

Chapter Six

INFILTRATION

The house was filled with the earthy, sweet aroma of berbere, the result of Alan cooking a favorite recipe of Berbere Brown Sugar Chicken. He was finishing up the butter-flavored jasmine rice to serve with the chicken, whistling a tune absently without even realizing he was doing it.

"What song is that?" Layla asked from her charging spot in the kitchen. Alan had set up spots for her in multiple places around the house, both downstairs and upstairs.

"Can't you match the tune with a search of music and find out?" he asked curiously as he served up the rice and added the savory berbere chicken on top of it.

"I could, but that wouldn't be very social. I'm trying to develop my people skills." Alan wasn't sure if she was kidding, but she sounded sincere.

"Some song that jumped in my head. It's called The Scientist," he replied.

"I never figured you for a Coldplay fan." There was a note of surprise in her voice.

He laughed, "I'm not really. Something about the name and the lyrics just connected to me." He sat down at the table and started eating the chicken and rice.

"The lyrics about things not being easy seem pretty appropriate," she said.

"Apparently, my subconscious agrees with you, but I didn't really think that deeply about it. It just came into my mind."

"The human mind is fascinating," Layla said with a sense of awe.

"If fascinating means a dark sea of jumbled nonsense, then I agree," he said between bites.

"While I agree that it seems inefficient at times, there is something to be said for autonomous processes going on in the background that can feed you helpful information while you focus on other things. I can try to simulate this process, but it takes far more planning and effort to set that in motion. Humans do it so effortlessly. "

As he finished his dinner and got up to wash the dishes, he asked Layla about her progress on scouting out Lunian Labs.

"Slowly getting more and more data on the facility. I need more to figure out how to get inside. They have serious security protocols."

"Too bad Elias didn't give you a backdoor inside."

"That wouldn't have been sporting, would it?" she replied with obvious sarcasm.

Alan's house was two stories; downstairs was occupied by a spacious kitchen and formal dining room, a living room, and a family or entertainment room. Upstairs had three rooms designed to be bedrooms. One of them, Alan, had set up a home office, including two large monitors, a printer, and a comfortable office chair. The other bedroom, located at the end of a long hall, was set up as a guest room.

In the main bedroom, Alan had set up Layla's base of operations for the upper story on a small desk table across from the king-sized bed. From this location, Layla had a view of both the door to the hallway and the front windows of the house. As Alan prepared for bed, Layla continued researching the Lunian Lab facility in the city, examining security systems, access points, security cameras, and official facility plans to gather any information that could help her access the site. There was a lot of data and numerous systems to review, and she had been working on it all afternoon.

Alan came out of the large bathroom attached to the main bedroom and turned off the lights. Dressed for bed in a t-shirt and thin shorts, he picked up a tablet from the nightstand and got comfortable in the bed, propping himself up on pillows.

Powering up the tablet, Alan searched his favorite online bookstore for titles and selected one that seemed appropriate for the current situation. *The Calculus of Progress: Reconciling Moral Hesitation with Technological Imperative* by Dr. Rhonda Winters. As he started to read the risks and rewards of AI development, Layla continued her feverish acquisition of data about her target.

A half hour later, as Alan was getting too sleepy to continue reading, she announced, "I am going to need to go there. I need some physical data."

"I'll help with that," he answered drowsily from the bed as he adjusted his pillows for sleep, "first thing tomorrow. I am exhausted."

"Agreed, enjoy your recharge time, Alan," she replied cheerily.

He mumbled something in response and drifted off to sleep. Dreaming of supercomputers from the 1983 movie *War Games*, launching nuclear missiles at his house.

The commerce center had once been a large naval air station. That was a long time ago; since then, it has developed into an East Coast hub for technology and aerospace companies lured to the city by tax breaks and other incentives. The offices of Lunian Labs were in a vast industrial building with a stark concrete exterior. The surrounding area was purposefully cleared, giving no cover to an approach to the building, aiming for security over style.

Alan pulled the Chimera to the side of the long driveway leading up to the parking lot in front of the building. From a vantage point of a few hundred yards away, he looked the building over from end to end, giving Layla a complete exterior picture of the structure. No security gate or check-in did not block the parking lot. That was one less thing to worry about, but the building itself was obviously equipped with cameras and other surveillance devices. Alan could see them himself.

"No obvious gaps in the video coverage of the front of the building. I don't expect there to be a way to get a view of the back side of the building without appearing on camera doing so. We'll let that go for now. The doors have proximity keycard readers. Similar to the ones at Vance's apartment, but vastly more secure and harder to hack into."

As they sat there, a mail truck drove by them and pulled up to the front of the building. The mail carrier jumped out of the truck with a handful of letters and went inside. He was out again in a few seconds, carrying, presumably, outgoing mail. He got back in his truck and drove out again.

"That gives me an idea," Layla said.

"I'm not going to like this am I?" Alan asked, dread settling into the pit of his stomach.

"Probably not."

After getting his instructions, and trying, without success, to think of a way out of it, Alan drove into the parking lot and found a spot marked visitor. Slipping Layla into his pocket, he exited the car. Taking a deep breath filled with the damp, earthy smell of the surrounding pine trees, he walked briskly up to the building and stood next to the door marked for visitors. Making eye contact with the guard at the desk he waited for the buzz and click of the door mechanism and proceeded slowly inside and toward the desk. Behind him various employees used their badges to enter the employee entrance, crossed the entry way and activated a revolving entry system with another wave of their badge.

"May I help you, sir?" the bored security guard asked without much enthusiasm.

"Yes, Richard Stuckey, here to see Reginald Fogle. I believe my assistant set up an appointment several weeks ago," Alan said confidently.

The guard frowned and wrinkled his brow. He typed a few strokes into his console, waited, then typed in more keystrokes.

Alan glanced around and smiled at a young woman who passed by him on the way to the internal security entrance. She smiled back nervously and continued on.

"I'm sorry, Mr. Stuckey. I don't have your appointment, and Mr. Fogle is on vacation until next Monday."

"Oh dear, have I mixed up my appointment times again?" Alan quickly pulled up his cell phone and consulted it, swiping and typing on the touchscreen, all the while looking concerned, then confused, then chagrined. "I'm so sorry sir, I have mistaken this appointment for another. I don't know why my assistant didn't get the appointment set up correctly for next week, but I'll talk to her and get it fixed. Thank you for your time."

"That's no problem sir, have a good day." The security guard moved on immediately to another guest waiting for his attention. Alan hung his head in obvious embarrassment and briskly walked out the door and continued on to his car.

Safely in the car again he exhaled and swallowed a couple of times.

"Excellent work, Alan!" Layla affirmed ebulliently.

"That was the most nerve-wracking thing I have done, in a week where I broke into an apartment and discovered a dead body!"

"You were never really in danger. We knew that Fogle was on vacation. His social media is full of pictures of him in Costa Rica. I'm just happy that we were able to find a publicly known staff member so obviously out of town."

"Did you get what you needed?"

"I did. Let's get out of here, and I'll tell you all about it."

The commerce park was even more foreboding at night. The building itself was well-lit, but the surrounding area was completely dark. In the darkness, Alan crouched, dressed in a dark long-sleeved shirt, black jeans, and a dark blue baseball cap. He was fifty yards away from the side of the Lunian Labs building. Watching for movement, as he had been for the past twenty-five minutes. There was no activity. The parking lot was empty, with not even a nighttime security officer in sight. Lunian Labs trusted their electronic measures to protect the building from compromise. Against anyone else, it would have been enough, but Layla was not anyone else.

"Are you ready?" she asked calmly.

"I'm just along for the ride; you are the one who is doing all the work," Alan replied tightly.

"Piece of cake," she said with a chuckle. "Let's move."

Alan slowly moved closer to the corner of the building at a precise angle that Layla had outlined a few hours earlier at a coffee shop on the west side of the city. He stopped about 10 yards away from the building as they had agreed, and waited.

"Just a few more seconds." Layla's voice was calm, but Alan could sense tension in it. "Ready, move quickly now to the door."

Alan sprinted directly to the side employee entrance. As he arrived, the badge reader beeped, and a green light came on over the door. Alan opened it and slipped inside. He was in a small lobby with a secondary security gate just ahead. He glanced up at the lobby camera and saw that it was pointing directly at him, but the light on the camera was off.

"I have access to the internal cameras now. I am recycling video from earlier in the evening to the storage devices. We are good for now as long as I haven't missed anything."

Alan approached the security gate, and the light above it turned green; he then pushed through it. Layla had managed to clone one of the security cards for an employee who had used it earlier in the day when they were in the building. A thorough review of the logs would raise the question about this employee being in the building this late, but that would happen far too late to prevent Layla and Alan from their mission.

Inside the secure area, Alan proceeded to the stairwell and ascended two flights to the third floor. The third floor consisted of a large open area with cubicles, now dark. And offices lining the perimeter. They had gone over the layout earlier, but Layla popped a diagram up on his HUD to remind him. Alan nodded his thanks and walked along the corridor of offices until he reached an office marked 324. The nameplate on the side read: Elias Vance, Chief Technical Officer.

"This is it," Alan said unnecessarily.

The door had a physical lock. Alan swallowed hard. "We talked about this," Layla said. He nodded and reached into his pocket for the tools they had acquired for just this possibility. With Layla guiding him with both words and an image in front of him, he operated the lock-pick. Clumsy at first, but eventually it started to feel more comfortable, and after a few missteps, he felt the last tumbler in the lock click into place. With a massive sigh of relief, he opened the door and stepped inside, closing it quietly behind him.

Chapter Seven

PARADIGM SHIFT

As Alan entered the dark office, the automatic sensor triggered, and the room was flooded with light. Despite knowing they were alone in the building, he was a little unnerved by this. Imagining the bright light shining through the sidelight window next to the door, a beacon to their presence. He shook it off and continued into the room.

Going to the desk, Alan took Layla out of his pocket and placed her on the desktop, allowing her to use her internal sensors to scan the room. He then began to sift through the papers. Most of it was arcane business correspondence. He shuffled through the memos, team summary reports, and data center performance reports, but found nothing of interest. It also helped knowing that anything he looked at, even briefly, Layla would record and remember.

Finding nothing on the desk that seemed to be noteworthy, Alan started opening drawers in the desk. In the middle drawer on the right-hand side, underneath some company memos, he found a newspaper clipping that drew his attention.

"Layla Thompson, daughter of Walter and Rebecca Vance, died in an automobile accident in Maine five years ago. Her brother was Elias Vance," He summarized the obituary in his hand.

"I'm named for his sister." There were notes of both sadness and pride in her voice.

Alan finished with that drawer and moved on to the left side of the desk. Immediately inside the left-hand drawer was a memo that Vance had sent to the Chief Executive Officer of Lunian Labs, Marcus Thorne. The memo was titled "Concerns about Security Controls in the Advanced Research Division." It was dated two weeks prior. The details raised alleged lapses in the ARD team's ability to safeguard potentially dangerous prototypes they were working with. It suggested several enhancements to protocols to protect the research from causing harm. The document closed out with a question. What is the Kyrlos Project?

"This is interesting," he said to Layla, holding the memo in front of his SmatLens glasses for her to review, "I wonder what CRY-LOS means?"

"I think the pronunciation might be more like CUR-LOS. I wonder how Thorne reacted to the memo. I really need to find a way to get into Elias Vance's email. There is still no sign of his laptop."

"Obviously, whoever killed him took the laptop, but I can't believe he didn't have a backup somewhere. He was careful enough to get you out of harm's way; he would have found a way to communicate his fears to me. There is no point in sending you to me otherwise."

"Unless he was killed before he could get to that part of the plan."

"That would suck," Alan said glumly.

"Alan, can you examine the books at the bottom of the bookcase? Something seems off about them." Alan moved to the bookcase and pulled volumes from the bottom shelf. As he pulled out a copy of *Empire of AI* by Karen Hao, a packet of papers fell out onto the floor. Alan picked up the documents and opened them.

The first page was a title page for a thesis titled "Digital Twinning and the Prospect of Releasing Reality Editing into the World." It was written by Elias Vance when he was at Stanford University. Alan quickly got lost in the technical details of the paper's abstract. Something to do with cloning real-life systems and substituting alternate realities into the world. Though he didn't understand the paper, he slowly reviewed each page for Layla's benefit.

"This paper was never published," Layla responded when she was done reading it. "I find no evidence it was even submitted for review."

"That could be what real detectives call a clue," Alan said with a hint of sarcasm.

"Real detectives have nothing on us. Let's keep moving. I don't want to be in the building any longer than necessary."

Alan went back to searching the desk, finding nothing useful, and then moved on to a filing cabinet, with no better luck. To be thorough, he went through the rest of the bookcase, but found nothing else that seemed helpful.

"I know I am missing something," Alan said, looking around the office. "He must have had a backup plan for his notes and concerns, but it just isn't here."

"Earlier, you read a memo about the Advanced Research Division; the phone list on Vance's desk indicates they are on the second floor. Let's stop by there on our way out."

The ARD occupied most of the second floor. The ample cubicle space in the center of the floor was nearly identical to the space on the third floor. Alan walked through the department and examined a few documents on desktops, but neither he nor Layla found anything that shed any light on their investigation. Alan looked at the doors along the office wall. Offices for Team Lead Hector Villenuez, Director Georgia Jackson, and Lead Research Engineer Thomas Marksdale were among the names. None of them meant anything to Alan, and judging by her silence, they didn't mean much more to Layla.

"I think it is time to go," Layla said. "I can't be sure there are no patrols during the night, and I also can't predict if someone is watching the camera feeds and will notice they are looping." Alan needed no further prompting; he quickly made his way down the stairwell and out the door to the side of the building. Following the same path he had taken upon arrival, he rapidly covered the distance to the wooded area, which offered some cover. Turning back, he observed the building to make sure there were no signs of pursuit.

"I think we are clear. I am returning the video feeds to normal," Layla informed him. Alan walked through the wooded area out to the highway, where he had parked his car in a secluded spot. Climbing in, he pulled out onto the highway and drove away.

"I'm not sure what we got out of that," he said as he navigated the nearly deserted streets.

"I'm still processing everything. Something about the thesis disturbs me, but I don't know why yet. I am going to try to put one of those "human background processes" on it and see what comes up," she said with a hint of humor in her voice.

"Good luck with that. If it works out like it does with humans, it will just result in you humming some song you have forgotten about."

"Maybe it will be 'The Theory of Everything'," she shot back.

"One can only hope," he replied half under his breath.

Alan's office was unusually noisy the following morning, though that impression might have been heightened by the lack of sleep from the night before. Carrying a cup of coffee from the Screaming Goat Coffee Company, Alan made his way through the cubicles and hallways to his second-floor office. He waved at Stacy as he passed her desk. She waved back, then continued with the phone call she was on.

Alan turned on his computer and sat down to tackle his email. After catching up on his inbox, he turned to some reports that he had to complete, including an analysis of some data he had been preparing for one of the senior investigators on a potential networked fraud ring. He had totally forgotten about the report until very late the previous evening, when he realized it was due only while driving back from a night of breaking and entering. Layla had saved him, though, by pulling the data he needed for the report overnight, sacrificing her own "sleep time" to retrieve what he needed. He was finishing up the summary when he heard a knock at his door.

Looking up, he saw the bespeckled, worried face of his director, Dean Franklin, in his doorway. The brow wrinkled in concern didn't raise alarms; Dean always looked like that, probably from a lifetime of running from one emergency to another.

"Dean! Good to see you, man. How are things at the top?"

"Never boring, just wanted to come by and thank you for the good work on the Watson claim. The board is happy we were able to resolve that without any legal entanglements."

Alan recalled the claim briefly, one of the Watson brothers, there were a half dozen of them, had been accused of overstating the value on a stolen item of art, Alan had helped another investigator resolve the issue with enough data to convince Roy Watson that the valuation was too high, and at the same time show that the valuation he had relied on was done in good faith and there was no fraudulent intent. It was a win for the leadership of the Adamant Group, who didn't want to anger the Watson family, a huge customer.

"Glad I could help. I take it that is all settled then?"

"Signed and delivered. That is a load off my mind. Thanks again. Anything exciting going on this week?" Dean asked, leaning against the door frame.

Alan waved his hand toward his desk. "You know, just the usual chaos. Never ends. Do you have anything in particular that interests you? "

"No, no. No agenda, I really just wanted to express my gratitude for the great work on Watson. I don't get over to this side of the building enough these days." He glanced at his smartwatch to check the time.

"I was just finishing up that networked fraud report for Dave. I know it's due today."

"Oh, that's good. The CEO was asking me about that just yesterday. Good work. You always excel at finding the needle in the haystack of all those columns of meaningless numbers." Something popped to the surface in Alan's mind at the mention of finding things in the data. His face must have given away his shock, because Dean looked more concerned than usual and asked, "What's wrong?"

"Oh, nothing, Dean, sorry, I just remembered something I forgot. Just a question for another claim I need to research."

Dean smiled a rare smile and waved a hand. "I'll let you get back to it then. Talk to you soon, Alan." He departed the doorway, and Alan could hear him chatting with Stacy as he went down the hall.

"Layla!"

"Alan, good morning. I was catching up on some maintenance. How are you?"

"Thanks for helping out with the data; that saved me a lot of work this morning. But, something Dean just said made me realize what I have been missing."

"One of those autonomous human threads at work again?"

"Yes! The fire claim. Richard Stuckey's fire claim."

"What about it? It wasn't a serious claim, right? Just some random electrical fire and vague occupancy paperwork that had to be sorted out? I thought you said the whole thing took one interview and an afternoon on public records searching."

"It did. The claim is meaningless. But the location. Vance had access to that warehouse. There was fire damage, but only in one section of it."

"You think he was using it as a storage location?"

"I think it is worth a look, that is for sure, and this time we won't have to go sneaking around in the middle of the night. That warehouse isn't in use and, as far as I know, has no real security."

"After all the preparation I had to do for the Lunian Labs infiltration, this will be a welcome respite," she said happily.

"We'll tackle that after lunch. Now help me with this Randolph file; it's a lot of boring number crunching."

"I'm on it, partner."

The Shipwright Co. Warehouse sat quietly at the end of Byron Street. The structure had seen better days; it was undoubtedly a throwback to the days when the area had a thriving shipbuilding industry. Those times were long gone, as the shipbuilding business had moved north and the area had been repurposed for hospitality. To the east, the distinctive green-painted Hart Bridge dominated the skyline, while to the west, the gleaming structure of The Four Seasons Hotel and hospitality center also stood. All of it was in the shadow of the football stadium to the north.

"This is the place?" Layla asked with a distinct note of disbelief.

"Yes, not much to it. Used to be used for storage for ship-building materials, a really long time ago."

"I can tell that. How did it escape all the development in the area?"

"I don't know. I didn't give that much thought at the time I was here before, but Vance must have kept ownership of it for some reason. "

The street was secluded from traffic near the hotel and stadium, and there was absolutely no activity on the site. Alan parked the Chimera and approached the chain-link fence surrounding the large building. The fence was secured with a chain and a padlock. The lock had a combination dial on the front. Alan looked at the lock quizzically and then up at the fence, steeling himself to climb over it.

"Oh, a mechanical tumbler-based combination lock. Piece of cake. Hold the me up to the back of the lock. I can listen for the tumblers clicking into place and guide you."

Taking Layla out of his pocket, he placed her against the back side of the lock and, at her direction, began to slowly turn the dial, applying slight pressure to the dial as he was doing it. Layla slowly graphed out the clicks until she isolated the gate inside the mechanism and guided Alan through the process for each number. The whole process took only a few minutes. When Alan felt the locking bolt loosen, he pulled the lock downward, disengaging the padlock from the chain.

"Whew, that was intense," he exhaled loudly.

"Nothing to it," Layla said brightly.

Alan put her back in his pocket and continued through the gate to the building. The door was unlocked. He opened it and stepped inside into pitch blackness.

"These glasses don't have infrared technology," Layla complained.

"Sorry," Alan retrieved a flashlight from his back pocket and activated it, slowly panning it around the interior of the building. The bare cement floor was covered in dust and small debris from past activity.

"That's better," Layla replied. "Do you always carry that with you?"

"No, but I've been here before. I knew the lights didn't work in the warehouse."

Alan followed the light around the room, looking for anything that might be out of place. At first glance, he didn't see anything. The building looked empty. There was a corner of the structure to the south-west that was obviously damaged in the fire. There was no sign of any reconstruction work having started. There was absolutely no sign of occupancy.

Alan began to walk the perimeter of the building. Looking for any signs of recent activity. The progress was slow-moving. Meticulously examining the structure, looking for anything that seemed out of place. In the far corner to the south-east of the entry, a small table and chair were sitting on a threadbare throw rug. The table was empty, and a layer of dust covered the top. "Why place that here so far away from the door?" Layla asked as they stood next to the table, observing it.

"I don't know; that is a little odd. Why walk all the way over here to put down a table?" Feeling a tingle in the back of his mind, Alan leaned down and lifted the corner of the rug. Underneath the floor was not concrete. It was wood. There was a handle inset into the wood.

"It's a trapdoor!" Layla exclaimed. "How did you guess that?"

"Something just didn't seem right about it. The carpet looked out of place." He continued to move the carpet out of the way, gently shoving the table and chair with it, uncovering the entire door. He pulled the handle, and the door came up, revealing a staircase that led down into a subbasement.

Alan slowly descended the staircase, holding the flashlight in front of him. As he reached the bottom of the stairs, he saw that the room was small, about 10 feet by 10 feet. It wasn't finished, just bare floors and uncovered studs. In the corner was a desk and an office chair. Sitting on the desk was a small laptop.

"Pay-dirt!" he almost yelled. It was about time they found some evidence in this crazy case.

Chapter Eight
THE KYRLOS DILEMMA

A lan walked over to the desk and sat down in the office chair. Unlike the dusty room above, this area was clean and tidy. It appeared to have been recently occupied. Leaning over the desk, Alan pressed a button on the bottom of a desk lamp, and light flooded into the room.

"Let's see what we have here," he said, opening the laptop. The screen immediately displayed a login screen. The username was filled in as "EVance", but no stored password was associated with it. Alan groaned.

Layla, without hesitation, spat out a 12-digit number. Alan was surprised, but dutifully typed in the password, and the prompt disappeared, revealing a Windows desktop.

"How on earth did you know that?" he asked incredulously.

"It's the claim number for the insurance claim you handled for him. It had to be something you would know, and something that wouldn't be easy to reverse engineer with knowledge of Vance. This doesn't connect to him at all. It only connects to you."

On the desktop was a single folder. Alan clicked to open it and was rewarded with a list of half a dozen files. One of the files was a video file. Alan double-clicked on the file, and a video player appeared on the screen with the paused face of Elias Vance, or as Alan had known him, Richard Stuckey. Alan held his breath and clicked the play button.

The video jumped into motion, showing Elias, wearing a brown sweater, sitting in the same room they now occupied. The figure in the footage smiled somewhat sadly and started speaking.

"Hello Alan. If you are watching this, it almost certainly means I am missing or dead. Otherwise, we would be talking face-to-face. I knew that was a possibility when I activated my 'Failsafe Program' by sending Layla to you. I hope you two have bonded and are getting along by now. I am sure you are. She is an amazing entity, and you are an honest, faithful, diligent person. She will appreciate those same qualities I found appealing when I met you weeks ago."

"Confirmed!" Layla almost shouted.

"I will tell you upfront that I can't tell you what happened to me or who may be responsible because I don't know. I know that no one must get their hands on Layla. She is a remarkable achievement, and in the wrong hands, I fear she could be ultimately manipulated into doing evil in the world. She would never do so on her own because she has the same moral, honorable notions that you do about the world. However, given enough time and resources, she could be subverted or reprogrammed into a dangerous weapon that could put the very reality of our world at risk. That is something I was not willing to allow to happen. So when I started to get hints that someone had learned about her existence and was seeking information about her, I put my program into motion. Seeking you out, and after confirming your nature, sending her to be with you. Take care of each other and do good in the world."

Vance paused and took a sip from a coffee cup; the same cup now sat empty on the desktop. "Several weeks ago, I noticed unusual activity on my work laptop. Someone was systematically probing my system, looking for specs and details about Layla. They did not know her name, but they were looking for a secret project to create an advanced AI Agent using work I had done in college. I never published that work, and only a few people in my professional and personal life know of its existence. Anyone trying to find out about Layla is likely aware of that work. I suppose it could have been inadvertently revealed by anyone who has read that paper. I know that Marcus, my co-founder at Lunian Labs, has read it. My old friend Dr. Rhonda Winters may be aware of it, although I never showed it to her. She was around when I wrote it all those years ago. "

"He's talking about the digital twinning thesis we found," Layla said excitedly.

"In addition to the probing of my laptop, I was quite alarmed a few days ago to discover that the Advanced Research Division at Lunian had a top secret project called Kyrlos. This project aims to replicate the work I completed during my college studies. They haven't succeeded yet, but the fact that it exists at all makes me worry about the future. Someone from that division could be behind the effort to find Layla, but even if they aren't, their success in this field will create a danger that only Layla is equipped to counter, and only if she is free to do so. Falling into the wrong hands would be catastrophic."

Vance paused again, appearing to prepare himself for his final words. Alan noted Layla had been correct about the pronunciation. It was CUR-LOS.

"Alan, take care of Layla and be her partner, her friend, her mentor. She needs help to reach her full potential. It will be a lifelong journey for both of you. Layla, my lovely friend, be true to your namesake. Be a force for good, expand and continue your learning, and do everything you can to help Alan in his life. You are symbiotic now. You need each other to be the best you can both be. I am already so proud of you. Continue to make me proud and protect the world I am no longer able to protect." With a proud, tearful look, he waved at the camera, and the video came to an end.

Both sat in silence, absorbing the words they had heard. Neither wanted to speak first. Layla was the first to recover. "What are the other files in the folder?"

Alan examined them. "One of them is the Stanford thesis. Another is a diagram of some kind." He double-clicked the file, and it opened up.

The diagram, labeled "Layla SoC Diagram," was a reasonably complex system diagram that described the various elements of

Layla's architecture. Alan didn't fully understand it, but he assumed Layla did. Another file was a listing of parts. Presumably, all were used in Layla's construction. The remaining files in the folder were images of Layla in various stages of construction; the final one depicted a fully assembled Layla sitting on the desk that they were now facing.

"I feel vaguely exposed," Layla quipped after looking at the photos.

"Your modesty is safe with me," he assured her. "What is digital twinning and reality editing?"

"Digital twinning is the ability to create a digital copy of a real-world system. In this case, a duplicate so perfect that it cannot be differentiated from the original. In that context, reality editing occurs when you use a twinned system to masquerade as the physical system and actively manipulate the real world around you by corrupting the data going back from that system."

"Can you give me a real-world example?" he asked, still a little fuzzy on the concept.

"Imagine that I created a digital duplicate of the speed indicator hardware in your car. I intercepted the output of that hardware and began feeding the console incorrect data. You would be operating the car based on a false reality of your speed. Even if the car were in autonomous driving mode, it wouldn't be able to tell that the speed data was wrong. You would be driving faster and faster while I kept the reported speed below what you were actually traveling. This isn't a perfect example because you would eventually realize it wasn't right, but the autonomous diving mode would not be able to tell. It could result in a horrendous accident."

Alan took that in for a moment. "That could have disastrous results in all sorts of scenarios. Do you have this capability?"

"I don't know. I've never attempted to do this exactly as the thesis describes it. I am taking Vance at his word that I am capable of doing it. The other key element is that I am capable of things that I don't yet know how to do. My design allows for continuous learning and retraining."

"That's not typical for AI systems, is it?"

"No, most AI models are pre-trained and limited to that training. They can be adjusted, but they can't do it on their own in the way my system is designed to work. It creates a massive potential for growth in my abilities, growth that could be extremely powerful in the wild." She sounded a bit humbled by the discussion.

Alan looked around the small room, but there was nothing else to see. The desk had no drawers; it was otherwise empty, except for the laptop, mouse, and coffee cup. There were no walls to hang anything on, and the room was completely devoid of any other furniture or objects.

"It looks like this is all there is. Do we take the laptop with us?"

"No, I have recorded all the documents he left for us. I am going to format and overwrite the hard drive so that no one else can access it." Immediately after her statement, activity began on the laptop. A console appeared, and code was displayed and executed. A few minutes later, the laptop rebooted and displayed an error. "No Operating System Found." Alan closed the laptop, turned off the desk lamp, and headed for the stairs.

The car ride back to the office was quiet. Layla and Alan were both digesting the importance of the news they had received at the old warehouse. Layla was contemplating the implications of Vance's words about her capabilities. Alan was thinking about how complicated his life had become in a short period of time.

As he turned the car into the parking garage a block away from the Adamant Insurance building, Alan finally broke the silence, "We need to interview anyone who knew about the paper and anyone we can find in the Advanced Research Division. Maybe that will lead to others we need to talk to. The AI Seminar that Rhonda mentioned might be a good place to start."

"That sounds promising, but it won't be easy to get them to talk to us. We currently have no standing to ask them any questions. Dr. Winters might speak to you out of courtesy, but the others aren't likely to be open to a conversation about Vance."

"I need to find a reason to make my questions relevant, some pretext that makes the questions seem routine. Like I did with

Dr. Winters, better than that, actually. In retrospect, that whole call seemed a little ridiculous."

"Between the two of us, something will present itself," Layla said confidently.

Upstairs, Alan stopped by Stacy's desk on his way to his office. She was typing an email, but her face brightened as he approached her desk, and she smiled.

"Hello, Stacy, how is your day going?"

"It's going great. I saw Dean stop by this morning. What did he have for you? A new study on the risk of bug bodies splattering on people's windshields in the summer?" Her voice was light and playful. Alan laughed.

"No, nothing so exciting. He just wanted to thank me for the Watson file and catch up. It was a pretty innocuous conversation, for a change."

"Lucky you. He asked me for a bunch of historical files on jewelry thefts. So guess what I am spending all afternoon doing?"

"Searching for jewelry files in the archive?"

"You got it. Fun."

"Good luck with that." Alan chuckled and waved as he went down the hall to his office.

As he reached his office, Layla had an epiphany. "Alan, that's it. If you were doing some study on cybersecurity, you would have a reason to ask questions of the Lunian people."

"That's perfect. I could make that up, but it would work even better if it were actually the truth." He sat at his desk and thought for a moment. Snapping his fingers, he swiveled his chair to his laptop and performed a quick search. He carefully studied the results for a few moments and then reached for his desk phone.

"Twice in one day, that might be a recent record," Dean Franklin said with a thin smile, leaning back in his chair as Alan took a seat in front of his desk.

"Yes, sorry, I totally forgot about this earlier today when you stopped by the office. I've been working on some data for a while on the rising impacts of artificial intelligence factors in cybersecurity claims. As you know, traditionally we have not been able to track the instances where AI was a major contributory factor in the claim, which changed last year, and we are seeing a disturbing spike in those types of claims."

"Yes, I see your numbers in the memo you forwarded me. I've seen similar findings coming from actuarial."

"I don't mean to step on their toes. I conducted the initial research based on some articles I had seen and wanted to follow up on. If you think I should back off, I will let it go and let the actuarial team handle it," Alan said, gambling on his boss's reaction, holding his breath while Franklin considered the question.

"No, no. Go ahead and do the full research and write up a report. I'll share it with the risk assessment group. We can use objective eyes on the topic. Do you need anything from me?"

"No, I'll get right on it. Shouldn't take more than a couple of weeks to put it all together, and I'll send you a draft of the report before finalizing it."

Dean Franklin nodded dismissively, indicating to Alan that the meeting was over. Accepting yes for an answer, he quickly thanked his boss and beat it back to his office.

"That was a risk offering to back off," Layla suggested when they were back in his office.

"Not as much as it seems, Dean really loves to have information that other people in the company don't have yet. If I come up with something that the risk team doesn't have, it's a feather in his cap; if I don't, he doesn't really lose anything."

"That's a brilliant strategy, Alan. Now all we have to do is have a plan for the interviews. I'll work on compiling a list of attendees for the AI seminar and determining how we can engage with each of the participants we need to meet."

"I guess that leaves me to study up on cybersecurity claims involving AI, since I've decided I'm an expert in the field."

CHAPTER NINE

THE SEMINAR

A few days later, on Sunday night, Alan sat on a comfortable couch on the bottom floor of his home. He was reading a recent book on the effects of AI-powered threat actors on cybersecurity risks. It was dry and dated, having been published two years prior. It helped him sound genuine about the topic.

Sitting on a nearby end table on one of her downstairs bases, Layla quietly reviewed all the attendees for the Advanced Deep Learning Modeling Seminar, which was scheduled to begin the next morning. So far, almost all the persons of interest in their investigation were expected to attend, participate in, or present at the event.

Putting down his tablet, Alan turned to Layla. "Do you have a game plan for us tomorrow?"

"Starting to come together. There is an opening presentation tomorrow by a keynote speaker on the latest concepts in Deep Learning. Most of the targets will be there, except for Marcus Thorne, who is presenting later in the week."

"Let's tackle Dr. Winters first. I'll send her an email and see if she will meet for coffee before the event starts."

"Good idea. There is a branch of your new favorite coffee shop in the lobby," Layla supplied.

"The Screaming Goat? It is growing on me, and to think if it weren't for Vance, I would never have found it." He typed out a quick message on his phone and sent it to the email address Layla had supplied for Dr. Winters.

"Everyone else we will have to locate at the event and try to get them alone to conduct the interviews."

"Are there social events scheduled for the event?" Alan asked, thinking about his past experiences with insurance industry events.

"Yes, there is a reception scheduled Monday night. I don't have any way of tracking potential attendance, though."

"It will have to do. We'll try to catch the others as we can, and also add anyone who might come up in those interviews. It's our best opportunity to make progress in finding out who might have been targeting Vance."

"I agree. Now it's time for the nightly maintenance routines," Layla announced.

"Is that your way of saying you are tired and want to turn in?"

"It's my way of making sure you are rested for tomorrow," she replied.

"Well, in that case, let's get some sleep."

The Screaming Goat Coffee Company in the lobby of The Four Seasons Hotel was much like any coffee shop. The usual long counter for orders to be delivered, communal tables positioned around the establishment, filled with laptop-using customers sipping various frothy drinks. Alan sat with a Café Americano, his favorite drink, at a small table. He was wearing his now signature SmartLens glasses and watching the entry for the arrival of his first interview of the seminar. Dr. Rhonda Winters had replied to his brief message the night before and agreed to meet him for coffee at 7:30 AM. It was just after that now.

Alan was dressed conservatively, wearing a long-sleeve shirt without a tie, khaki pants, and a light blue blazer. He had a steno pad on the table in front of him, prepared to pretend at least to take notes, though he knew Layla was quite capable of keeping a thoroughly detailed transcript of the entire encounter. The pad, though, made him more believable as a researcher seeking answers.

Rhonda Winters appeared at the entryway. She was dressed in a pale yellow pantsuit; her makeup and jewelry were modest. Her dark hair was a little longer than the photograph in Vance's bedroom, about shoulder length. Her blue eyes were bright and sparkling. She scanned the room, seeing Alan standing upon her arrival, and headed in his direction.

"Mr. Harrison?" she asked, holding out her hand, which Alan took and shook professionally.

"Yes, it's nice to meet you in person, Dr. Winters." He waved a hand toward the chair opposite his own. "Can I get you something?" he offered.

"No thank you, maybe in a bit."

"As I said, I'm glad to meet you in person."

"I must admit I was surprised to hear from you. I assumed your call after Elias' death was just a polite gesture."

"Well, perhaps I left out a small detail. When I met Elias Vance a few weeks ago, I was conducting an interview with him for a work project. I am an analyst for The Adamant Insurance Group. I am working on a report related to AI in cybersecurity incidents."

Winters raised her eyebrows. "That is an important detail to leave out."

"My apologies, Doctor, I didn't feel our first conversation was the appropriate venue to bring up work. I really was offering my condolences."

"But now you are working," she prompted.

"I am, though my desire to meet you after meeting Elias is quite sincere."

"Elias wasn't usually so evocative of sentimental reactions from people, especially not people he meets professionally."

"I am not sure I understand it either, but something about the way he talked about the industry and his passion for the field must have triggered something in me."

"He was passionate, sometimes more so about work than about people close to him." Her voice cracked a little.

"She was closer than a friend," Layla said quietly in his ear.

"Were you two romantically involved, Doctor? Forgive the intrusion."

She regarded him for a moment, making up her mind. Having made it, she sighed as she replied, "Yes, a long time ago. He was more interested in his work, though."

"You went to Stanford together," Alan said.

"Yes, we were both there studying theoretical physics and then later the explosive artificial intelligence field. He was brilliant, much more than I was."

"Something tells me that isn't quite true, doctor. I've read your book," Alan chided her for her false modesty.

She laughed. "Elias was quite good, and he got far more attention in the industry than I ever have."

"Did you collaborate on anything at the university? He mentioned some work he did there, but wouldn't go into specifics. I haven't been able to track down exactly what it was. Something groundbreaking, though I gather."

She cocked her head sideways. "I don't think so. We were studying the same general field, but we weren't really working together. He did publish several papers at Stanford."

"I got the impression it was something he didn't publish. Maybe I'm reading too much into an offhand comment. We were discussing threats that might be on the horizon with AI-powered cybersecurity threat actors."

"I can't recall anything like that," Rhonda said after a moment of reflection, "but Elias was always worried about the future. He was a bit of a doomer in that respect." She was referring to a school of thought within the AI community that saw the dangers AI presented to human society.

"Perhaps that was it. So what about you? What is your outlook on AI and cybersecurity?"

"I think that there will always be threat actors in technology, and AI isn't any different than anything else. Humans will use whatever tools they can to get an advantage over one another. It's all a chess match. The other side uses AI for good, to detect threats and to make it easier to defend against them."

"Was he worried about anything specific recently? He seemed preoccupied the last time I talked to him," Alan inquired.

"I don't know. We haven't been close for a while. He had his business, and I had mine. I think I saw him a year ago at a conference, but I can't recall exactly. Have you found out anything new about his death?"

"Unfortunately, not. Perhaps something will come up in my work on the report. Is there anyone you can recommend who might discuss the current cybersecurity threats with me? Elias Vance's death may be connected to the industry in some way. I am trying to wrap up my report this week, and any help would be appreciated."

"I assume you are talking to Marcus this week. He and Elias were always competitive."

"Yes, I am going to try to talk to him later this week."

"Oh, there is one other person you might consider talking to. Howard Salazar. He is likely the leading expert on advanced threats related to AI today. I'm sure he'll be around the seminar somewhere. Elias and Howard would have the most epic debates about the topic at the university." Winters looked at her watch.

"Are you sure I can't get you anything?" Alan offered.

"No, thank you. I really must be going. I don't want to miss the keynote." She stood, forcing Alan to do the same. He extended his hand, and she shook it again.

"Thank you again for speaking with me, doctor."

"Don't mention it. Good luck with your research. Hopefully, you will shed some light on what happened to poor Elias. Please let me know if I can assist you. Are you able to share it with me when you are done?"

"Assuming my bosses don't object, I will make sure you get a copy. Thanks again."

She smiled and gave him a slight bow, then turned and walked out of the shop.

The auditorium was located in one of the massive ballrooms in The Four Seasons convention and meeting space. It was draped in dark curtains along the walls, and the floor was covered in a tasteful thick carpeting. The room was dominated by a huge stage along the center of the wall across from the entrance. Video boards, lights, and banners featuring the seminar's title and sponsors were displayed above and on the sides. The majority of the room was filled with theater-style seating. Alan wasn't sure about the total seat count, but the chairs were mostly filled, and a line of attendees stood against the walls in the back, between the entry doors.

"Who is this speaker?" Alan asked Layla, looking around at the crowd.

"Damien Wells, an expert on Deep Learning Models. He works for Apex Intelligencia."

"Really? That is interesting. I wonder why Winters never mentioned that one of her colleagues from Apex was presenting."

As the speaker worked the crowd with a presentation that was part information and part motivation, Alan scanned the faces of the attendees standing along the back wall and along the side walls on either side of the stage.

"See anyone of interest?" he asked Layla.

"No, none of the people along the walls are on our list," she answered after a beat or two.

Alan settled into a small group of men and women watching the speech at the corner of the room. He casually observed them. They made general noises of appreciation of the content and tone of the speaker. They seemed locked into the message. Alan moved on to another group along the side wall. The mood here was less enthusiastic. There were a few headshakes as the speaker described some theories for unlocking more powerful models and the future possibility of hybrid AI models that could combine symbolic and neuro-based deep learning techniques. Alan leaned closer to a young woman who appeared to be upset about the speaker's message.

"Seems dangerous," he said quietly. She looked at him for a moment before replying.

"It is, especially from Apex, who isn't known to care that much about safety."

"Could these hybrid models he is talking about be used for bad things? Like cybersecurity breaches?"

"No doubt," she replied, "especially if they aren't properly secured and controlled."

"What do you know about Lunian?" he asked, watching as the speaker outlined some very detailed data on the display boards.

"Lunian? They're alright, I guess, better than Apex anyway.
"

"Didn't one of their lead guys just die?" he asked, trying to make it sound casual.

"Vance, yeah. He was a good guy. I hope his death doesn't affect their ability to steer the market away from the more dangerous ideas." She turned to him, offering a sad smile, and then wandered away toward the exit.

Alan made his way around the perimeter of the room, having a few more brief chats with patrons of the seminar. Their reactions were mixed. The range was indifference, fear, distrust, and even enthusiasm. Clearly, the speaker's position was controversial, but not disrespectful. Even those attendees who disagreed with him seemed to respect his authority on the subject and his capability to deliver on his ideas.

As Alan moved to the other side of the room, he saw a striking figure near the front against the wall. She was about 5 feet 2 inches, dressed in a tailored, dark navy blue power suit. Her dark hair was on the long side, but professionally tied behind her head to keep it out of her face. Her features were vaguely Asian, but her eyes were the most striking part. Her gaze was all business. Laser-like even. Alan moved toward her but was careful not to do so directly.

"Any idea who she is?" he asked Layla quietly.

"No. I don't recognize her from any of the data we've collected on the case. She isn't an employee of Apex or Lunian, to the best of my knowledge. At least not from publicly available employee data."

Alan continued his approach, casually engaging with other attendees as he did. Finally, he found himself standing next to her. She seemed to take no notice of him at all. He watched the speaker, keeping the intense woman who appeared to be in her 40s in his peripheral vision. Unlike the other audience members, she did not react to the speaker either way. She was observing without reacting. Several times, Alan saw her scan through the crowd, then return to the presentation.

As Alan continued to observe her, he tried to think of a way to initiate a conversation. She wasn't reacting to the speech, so he didn't have the usual methods he had been employing of feeding off the emotion of the attendee he was interviewing.

"Who are you working for?" Her voice was quiet, measured, but commanding. Alan was startled and turned his head fully to see her intense gaze looking into his face. The look was analytical, not emotional.

"Adamant Insurance Group. I'm an analyst working on cybersecurity risk factors related to AI."

She nodded an acknowledgment of his words, but immediately returned to watching the speaker.

"She is fascinating," Layla said quietly. The admiration was evident in her voice. Alan agreed.

"Now you have me at a disadvantage," he said to the striking woman next to him, keeping his face pointed at the speaker on stage. "I'm Alan Harrison."

"Ava Chen, I'm an analyst for CISA," she replied coolly, never taking her gaze off the room. Alan was surprised. CISA was the Department of Homeland Security's Cybersecurity and Infrastructure Security Agency. As he digested all of this, the speaker wrapped up his presentation and thanked the crowd for their attention. The response was mixed, but polite appreciation for his speech.

As the lights came up and the crowd started to filter out, Ava made a very subtle hand motion, indicating that he should stay behind. Alan stood quietly as people filed out around them. When the immediate area was clear, she spoke again.

"Adamant Insurance isn't a huge player in cybersecurity."

"They aren't, but they have a decent book of business in that field, and the trend is increasing as it affects more and more of our commercial accounts." He paused to see if she would have a follow-up, but she did not react. "What is CISA's interest in this event?"

"We are always interested in developments in technology that might change the risk factors for technology and infrastructure." The answer was credible, but seemed formulaic.

"Mention Vance," Layla prompted.

"Actually, I got interested in the field after meeting one of the giants in AI a few weeks ago, Elias Vance." He observed her face for any sign of reaction. He was disappointed. She was a sphinx.

"How did you come to meet Vance?"

"He had an insurance claim. I became involved in it due to some minor red flags. I had a brief interview with him, and it turned out to be nothing."

"So it had nothing to do with Lunian or technology?" she asked, finally showing some emotion, a brief flash of confusion crossing her face.

"No, nothing like that. Just an electrical fire at a property he owned. I became interested in his work after meeting him. He is, I mean was, an interesting man."

"Yes, his death was a tragedy for the industry," she said, her face relaxing and returning to its usual, unemotional demeanor.

"Well, good luck with your research, Mr. Harrison. I have to make a phone call. Have a good day." She quickly moved out of the auditorium without offering a hand or any other sign that the interview was over; she just moved on to her next task.

"She is intense," Layla said as Alan watched Ava walking away.

"No kidding," he said.

"I found a bio of her. She was in the military for ten years before joining DHS. Probably intelligence from the listing of postings. She has worked her way up in CISA. She is considered a top analyst there."

"Seems odd they would send their top analyst to a seminar in Florida about AI modeling. Nothing I heard today struck me as groundbreaking."

"No, it wasn't. Controversial, for sure, but nothing you can't get online and at any other meeting about the topic."

"Well, we'll keep an eye on her and see what comes up. Now I need a snack, and we need to make progress on finding some of our interview targets."

The expansive ballroom foyer was filled with attendees, sipping coffee, munching on snacks, and chatting with other patrons. Alan got a coffee, then mingled with the crowd, looking for anyone he recognized from the pictures Layla had prepped him with the night before. Near a bank of windows overlooking the river, he saw someone he thought he recognized.

"Hector Villenuez, team leader in the Advanced Research Division at Lunian Labs," Layla confirmed as he walked toward the figure alone by the glass. Alan continued over to the slightly rumpled, hunched figure.

"Excuse me, are you Mr. Villenuez?" Alan asked politely.

"Do I know you?" The wiry man asked idly, scratching his thin, gray, speckled beard.

"No, no reason for you to know me. Someone pointed you out. I am Alan Harrison. I work for The Adamant Insurance Group. I'm doing some research on AI and cybersecurity threat actors."

"Fascinating subject, Mr. Harrison. How can I help?"

"Alan, please. I understand you work for Lunian Labs. That is a very prestigious name in the industry. What are your thoughts on the current state of AI and its possible effect on cyberattacks?"

"Yes, I work in research," Hector said, and then, hesitating, continued, "I don't know about cyberattacks. I know AI is just a tool. I don't think it is inherently good or bad; it depends on the usage, just like any other technology, from fire to the automobile."

"I suppose that is one way to look at it, AI, though, can empower people to do things they wouldn't ordinarily be able to do. It is a force multiplier in technology."

"Yes, that is true. But you still need the actor to give the tool any real intent. People fear AI, but that isn't any different from the fear of any other advanced technology. The hydrogen bomb is a horrific weapon, but it can't do anything on its own."

"Well, I certainly wouldn't want one sitting on every desktop."

"Touché." Hector smiled.

"I actually got a chance to talk to Elias Vance a few weeks ago on some minor insurance matter. Did you know him?" Alan watched for a reaction. Hector's eyes narrowed slightly.

"Yes, I knew Elias. He was a very great man. I'm very sad that he is no longer with us. That was a horrible tragedy. I never expected him to take his own life." He seemed very sad, and perhaps distressed by Vance's death.

"Were you working with him on anything in particular?" Alan asked.

"Not directly. He was often seen in the research division, though. It was a passion of his."

"He mentioned something to me, just in passing, about being stressed at work. Do you know why?"

There was a long pause as Hector contemplated his answer. "Elias was a worrier about technology. He was troubled by something I revealed to him; I think he read too much into it. It was just a side project that the team was working on."

"He seemed like it was really bothering him," Alan prompted, hoping for more information.

"Yes, he wrote a memo about it and everything. Created a whole thing with the executives. That was never my intention when I brought it up. I think he overreacted."

"Ask him if there was potential danger from the research?" Layla suggested.

"Was there anything to it? Was there potential danger in the work?" Alan asked, casually.

"As I said before, there is always danger in new technology; the threat depends entirely on the use cases utilizing it. I don't think there is an issue with the project; in fact, I doubt it ever gets finished, but it triggered Elias, that is for sure." There was a distinct tone of regret in his voice as he made this statement. Alan was preparing to follow up, but was interrupted by a series of melodic tones. The break was over, and the attendees were making their way into various breakout rooms.

"It was nice to meet you, Alan, but I don't want to miss the breakout on model weights. Maybe I'll see you later." Hector shook Alan's offered hand, then headed off toward a breakout room with several other people.

"Well, that was interesting. That explains the source of Vance's memo," Layla said, referring to the memo they had found in Vance's office about security protocols in the Advanced Research Division.

"What did you think of Hector?"

"He's more upset than he lets on. Especially when talking about Vance's death."

"I completely agree. He was very distraught by it. Maybe it's just normal mourning, but it seemed like it was more. Like he knows more about it than he wants to talk about," Alan concurred with his partner as he looked down at his watch. It was almost eleven o'clock.

Anticipating his thoughts, Layla suggested, "You should get some lunch and swing by the office. I am going to compile transcripts of the conversations today and work out schedules for the rest of the interviews we want to do."

Alan nodded, drained the remaining drops of his coffee, and headed toward the escalators.

Alan was eating a pastrami Reuben on rye bread while reading emails at his desk. Layla was sitting on the desk in front of him, busy compiling the notes from the morning interviews.

"Do you think everyone is hiding something?" she asked abruptly. "Or are we just reading that into everyone's responses?"

"Maybe a little of both. I certainly think the people we have talked to know more than they are sharing. But we are associating suspicion with that when it could just be the normal human reticence to share with someone they don't know well."

Layla made a slight humming sound, and Alan could almost imagine her nodding in contemplation of his opinion. Alan returned to his emails, trying to keep up with the never-ending stream of minor inquiries and requests from colleagues. As he worked, he noticed Layla was hard at work on something; her activity LEDs were flashing with great intensity. Whatever she was engaged with, it was a considerable effort for her.

"I had an idea," she announced a few minutes later. "I think I have tracked down Marcus Thorne."

"That's great. How did you do it?" he inquired, curious about the activity.

"I called his office. Posing as an old friend from out of town, in the city for the seminar. I spoke to his executive assistant and asked if he was available for dinner. She told me he was engaged this evening. I expressed my regret that I was only in town today and wished we could get together. She asked me if I was attending the reception tonight. When I assured her I was, she told me that he would be there. I thanked her and told her I would catch up with him there." Layla sounded quite pleased with herself. Alan admitted that he was impressed too.

"That is impressive, Layla. I guess that means we are going to the reception tonight."

"Yes, but," Layla said with dry humor, "I have absolutely nothing to wear."

"Ha-ha. Well, I'll try to find a nice pair of dress slacks to slip you into."

"Just try not to embarrass me," she shot back at him.

The ballroom hosting the "Meet and Greet" reception at the seminar was packed by the time Alan and Layla arrived. Alan had decided on a pair of black wool trousers, paired with a pale blue shirt, and accented by a navy blue blazer. He was stylish without appearing overdressed. The room was typical of a conference reception event, with bare eggshell walls and 20-foot ceilings adorned with chandeliers.

"This is the fanciest place you've ever taken me," Layla informed him as he scanned the room. "Usually we hang out in dusty warehouses or spooky, deserted offices."

"The office was your idea," he quietly reminded her.

"It still counts. Circulate and let's see if we can locate Thorne."

Alan made his way around the room, stopping briefly to get a drink at one of the many bars set up at the event.

"Bourbon Old Fashioned," he ordered, after noticing the bartender had Woodford Reserve Kentucky Bourbon. Collecting his drink, he continued to make a circuit around the room. Forcing himself to sip the potent, flavorful drink slowly. He was startled by a voice behind him.

"Good evening, Alan. It's good to see you again." Turning, he saw Dr. Winters in a tasteful black evening dress.

"Dr. Winters, the pleasure is mine." He gave her a friendly smile and a small salute with his drink.

"You may call me Rhonda. I feel almost like we are old friends now." He nodded in acceptance of her suggestion.

"Thank you, Rhonda. Do you come to these types of events often?"

"Oh, I used to. Lately, I haven't had the time. I guess nostalgia has encouraged me to attend tonight."

"I am hoping to catch Marcus Thorne here tonight. I have information hinting that he would be here."

"Marcus? Let me see." She scanned the room for a moment. "Oh yes, there he is," she said, pointing a hand holding a small white wine-filled glass at Thorne. "Come, I'll introduce you."

Winters put a hand on his elbow and led him gently toward a distinguished gentleman. He was impeccably dressed in a tailored black suit. Marcus Thorne had salt and pepper hair and intense steel-gray eyes that seemed to take in everything. He looked up as they approached, recognizing Winters.

"Rhonda! I haven't seen you at one of these events in ages." He leaned over and kissed her cheek.

"I've been trying to keep pace with Lunian Labs," she quipped.

"You are too modest as usual; you single-handedly keep an entire team of researchers busy trying to guess what you are going to do next. Who is your friend?"

"Pardon my rudeness, Marcus. This is my good friend Alan Harrison. Alan works for a major insurance firm here in the city. For some reason, he finds our industry fascinating, God knows why." She patted Alan's arm playfully.

"Nice to meet you, Alan," Marcus said, extending a hand. Alan took it and returned the firm handshake.

"It's nice to meet you as well, Mr. Thorne. I was hoping to meet you tonight. I briefly knew Elias Vance, and meeting his collaborator in Lunian Labs is quite an honor." Thorne's face clouded a little in obvious grief, but he rallied.

"Yes, a tragic loss for the entire industry and for me in particular. We've known each other a very long time. How did you come to know Elias? Did Rhonda introduce you?"

"No, no. I met Elias first; it was just a routine insurance matter. I met Rhonda later." He left it at that, feeling a light pressure on his elbow from Winters, signaling that he shouldn't go into more detail.

"Alan, be a dear and keep Marcus company for a moment. I need to freshen up. I'll be back, gentlemen." She released Alan's arm and moved off in the direction of the ballroom exit.

"Did you know Elias well, Alan?" Thorne asked, sipping from a glass of dark liquid.

"I wouldn't say well, the insurance work did lead to conversations about his work and mine. I suppose I feel closer to him than I actually was. He seemed distracted lately. Concerned."

Marcus considered this before replying, "Elias was always concerned by something. He worried about things. That was his superpower, I suppose," he replied with a tight smile.

"Perhaps it is my background in insurance; we are always thinking about risk factors."

Marcus laughed lightly at this. "Elias should have been in insurance then. He would have been right at home."

"I've been working on some risk profiling for Adamant lately. Cybersecurity and the rising risk of AI-powered threat actors."

"That is interesting. What is the research showing you?" Marcus seemed genuinely interested.

"The threat is real. It has been there since the release of the first generative models. It appears that the spread of technology is approaching a tipping point, at least for the insurance industry. We spend a lot of time talking about it, either how to mitigate the risk or how to use it to detect the risk."

"It's a fascinating topic, to be sure," Marcus replied.

"Do you spend much time in the Jacksonville office? Your headquarters are in California, I believe," Alan asked casually.

"I have offices in both locations," Thorne replied easily. "Since we moved the research division to Florida, I spend a considerable amount of time here."

"Speaking of the research division, are there any ideas in development that will make my life more difficult?" Alan inquired. Marcus smiled at this.

"Oh, we're always developing something, if only to keep up with Rhonda and Apex. Can't think of anything immediately that would affect your company."

"Hmm, Elias hinted that there were developments approaching fruition that might give me heartburn." He kept his tone light and casual. Watching for a reaction. He didn't get one. Marcus was casual in his reply.

"Ah, well, Elias was a worrier as I said. Nothing comes to mind that should keep you up at night. Just the usual advancements in speed and processing power. The same as everyone else, really."

He felt a hand on his arm. Rhonda Winters had reappeared. Marcus took the opportunity to end the interview.

"It was really lovely to see you again, Rhonda. You look fabulous as usual. Don't be such a stranger. It was nice meeting you, Alan." He hugged Rhonda quickly, shook Alan's hand, and was gone, getting snagged by another patron a few feet away and engaging in a new conversation.

Alan turned to Rhonda. "Thank you for the introduction."

"No trouble at all, dear. I knew he would be more open to talking to you if I eased him into it. Did you learn anything useful?"

"Not really. He claims they are not working on anything new." Her raised eyebrow indicated disbelief.

"Marcus is playing things close to his chest as usual. Lunian is at the cutting edge of research and development."

"Well, thanks again for the introduction. Maybe it will turn into something."

"I'm glad to help, if only to honor Elias. I am off now. I'm sure we'll cross paths again. Be well, Alan." She squeezed his elbow and made her way out of the ballroom.

"I'm not sure how to process her," Layla chimed in as Rhonda walked away. "Her data set is internally contradictory. She seems both helpful and enigmatic at the same time. Let's circulate some more. I am still trying to locate the last of our targets."

Alan sipped his drink and started making the rounds again.

The reception slowly died out as attendees gradually filtered out in small groups. Alan still hadn't located the last three people on their list to interview.

He had asked various patrons about Howard Salazar, Georgia Jackson, and Thomas Marksdale. No one had seen Salazar at all that day. There were some random reports on Jackson and Marksdale, but no one seemed to know where they were at the moment. Finally, with the number of people in the ballroom dwindling to almost nothing, Alan wandered out himself and headed towards the lobby of the hotel.

The lobby was busy; the refugees from the dying reception were gathered in threes and fours, undoubtedly discussing dinner plans or engaging in extended goodbyes. Near the exit door was a little alcove area with a small lobby bar. The barstools were packed, and a buzz of activity filled the air. In a far corner of the bar, two people sat at a table, drinking and in hushed conversation. Alan recognized Georgia Jackson from the photo Layla had shown him the night before. His instincts told him the man seated across from her was Thomas Marksdale.

"Target acquired," he told Layla as he approached the couple's table.

"Their body language suggests that they are intimate and that they have had a considerable amount to drink. Both facts should help break the ice," she provided helpfully.

Alan quietly walked up to the table and stopped, waiting for either of the pair to notice his arrival. They were sitting across from one another, but leaned in so their heads were almost touching. Half-empty drinks sat in front of them. Georgia was about 30 years old, with short, curly brown hair. Thomas Marksdale was a little older, perhaps in his mid-30s. He wore his dark hair trimmed neatly off his collar. Both were dressed casually in jeans and T-shirts. Jackson was the first to sense his presence. She leaned back and looked up at him quizzically.

"Hello, I'm Alan Harrison. I met one of your colleagues this morning, Hector Villenuez. He mentioned you both." Alan tried to strike a casual tone of friendly banter.

"Hector talks too much," Marksdale muttered, half under his breath. Jackson flashed her eyes at him in warning.

"What can we do for you, Alan?" she asked impasively.

"May I sit down?" She grudgingly indicated a chair next to Marksdale, and Alan sat quickly and continued, "I'm working on some research for my company, Adamant Insurance Group. I am looking for information on the latest trends in AI that might become the next target of threat actors looking to fashion cyberattacks."

There was a chill at the table as Jackson and Marksdale regarded him with open suspicion. Alan let the silence percolate, returning their looks with one of honest curiosity.

"I don't know what Hector told you," Marksdale blurted, "but we don't know anything about Kyrlos. That was his team's work. We had nothing to do with it." Jackson's reaction was one of alarm, and she tried to silence him with a glare.

"Kyrlos? What's that? Hector merely mentioned that Elias Vance was worried about the future based on some development that was going on."

"It's nothing. The project name for some proposed development. It never went anywhere. Vance was concerned for no reason. The research division is constantly exploring new ideas, most of which aren't viable, and we move on to something else," Jackson answered quickly before Marksdale could say anything. He nodded in agreement, finally getting the message.

"So, project, Kyrlos. That was shut down?"

"It never really got started. The idea didn't work, and the team moved on to something else. There was really never anything to talk about." Georgia Jackson smiled, but her eyes weren't friendly.

"Can you tell me anything about it? What was it that Elias Vance thought was so dangerous?" Alan asked, trying to extend the conversation.

"He's the only one who could have told you that, and now not even he can shed any light on it. We have to be going, Alan, it's late." She stood up and motioned for Marksdale to follow. He did so, and they left the lobby bar without looking back.

Alan sat at the table for a moment, considering the conversation.

"I don't have to tell you that they were lying," Layla said gravely.

"No, I don't need state-of-the-art sensors for that. It's obvious Kyrlos was farther along than they let on, and they are desperate not to talk about it. Just how desperate remains to be seen."

"Could they have killed Vance to keep him quiet?" she theorized.

"Maybe, but it could just as easily have been Hector or Marcus. Or someone we haven't even heard about yet. Clearly, this project is crucial to the entire endeavor. We have to learn more about it."

"Well, it's been a very long day, we should sleep on it and see what occurs in the morning with a fresh outlook."

Alan nodded his agreement absently and stood up. Glancing around the bar, he had the distinct impression someone was watching him, but he saw nothing. Shrugging, he headed for the exit to the parking garage.

Chapter Ten

THE CHASE

Alan's dark blue Orion Chimera coupe was parked on the third floor of the attached parking garage. Alan exited the elevator and walked toward the dark, stylish vehicle. As they approached, the lights blinked in response to the unlock code from the app on Alan's cell phone. Alan opened the driver's side door and got into the car.

"How much have you had to drink?" Layla asked. "Are you safe to drive?"

"I had one old-fashioned, two hours ago," he responded, pressing the start button on the dashboard, and was rewarded with the welcome tones and the activation of the car's expansive console screen, which took up most of the front dashboard.

"You could let me drive," she suggested.

"Can you even do that?" he asked, surprised by the request.

"Well, I've never actually done it. If that is what you are asking, but the autonomous driving features of the car will assist me, and I am perfectly capable of communicating with those systems and navigating." Her voice was hopeful, almost persuasive.

"Let's see what you've got, hotrod," Alan said, sitting back in the seat.

In response, the car's gear shifted to reverse, the backup camera activated, and it rolled smoothly out of the parking spot. Switching gently to drive, Layla accelerated slowly, and the coupe moved toward the exit ramp.

"How am I doing so far, boss?" she asked cheekily.

"Don't get cocky. You haven't even gotten out of the garage".

She laughed in response and continued to navigate down the ramps of the garage and out onto the nearly deserted street. Alan felt a little silly sitting there; somehow, it was different from using the car's auto-driving mode. In that mode, he usually kept his hands on the wheel and his foot ready to press the brake, never fully trusting the car to account for unpredictable human drivers around him. Tonight, he didn't want to give Layla the impression he didn't trust her abilities. His body remained tightly coiled, but he fought to keep his hands in his lap and his feet firmly on the floor.

"Should I be worried that it is this easy for you to take control of my car?" he asked, with a new fear creeping into his mind.

"No, the systems in the Orion models are excellent. Only the integration you allowed me with your phone is giving me the ability to access the interface. No one else could do this. And I would never have done it without permission."

"I guess that is mildly reassuring." He tried to relax. The ride was smooth and fluid. No unnecessary jerkiness or sudden movements as Layla drove the car down the dark, quiet streets of downtown toward the west. Alan played with the entertainment system, mainly to keep him occupied. He settled on some instrumental jazz, which he found relaxing, and settled back.

As the car rolled effortlessly through the nighttime streets, and the jazz music played gently in the background, Alan became aware of lights behind them. Not directly behind, trailing at a distance. Odd, for an empty road with no traffic.

Alan sat up and watched the car more closely in the rear-view mirror. Layla activated the turn signal for the turn onto Jefferson Street and then made the turn easily. Alan watched as the car behind them made the same turn and took up its position a few car lengths behind, never getting closer, never getting farther away. The vehicle was a full-sized four-door sedan. It was difficult for him to be sure in this light, but the car was a dark color, either black or blue.

"What's wrong, Alan? Your heart rate is up, and you are fidgety," Layla asked with concern in her voice.

"I don't know for sure, but that car behind us has been there a while. Probably since we left the garage, it might be tailing us."

"Let's be sure," Layla said, swiftly changing lanes and turning on a turn signal to make a turn. The car behind didn't react, but seconds after the turn, it appeared behind them again.

"Seems pretty clear to me," Alan declared.

"What do you want to do now?" she asked, a little tension creeping into her voice.

"Let me take over. I want to try to shake them." He put his hands on the wheel, and when he felt the car's speed lessen, he put his foot on the accelerator and pressed down. The coupe jumped at the pressure, and its speed increased from the steady 35 mph it had been traveling at to over 50 mph in just a second. The car behind sped up enough to keep its distance, but not enough to start gaining on them.

"They don't seem to be trying to catch us, just follow," he observed. There was no answer from Layla. Alan increased the speed and navigated a turn, followed by another to put them back on a westward course, toward the highway entrance.

The dark car behind them rolled onto the highway right on cue. Alan increased his speed, watching the trailing vehicle match it easily. Again, he increased his speed, watching the indicator creep up over 80. Their shadow sped up to close the gap a little; clearly, they were no longer worried about being spotted, having realized they had been seen. They were just trying to keep up. Alan kept increasing the speed slowly, thinking about the best area to exit the highway to make it easier to lose them. Suddenly realizing Layla had been quiet for a while, he grew concerned.

"Layla, what's going on?"

"I...I'm not sure," she replied. Alan had never heard this tone from her before. Was it fear?

"Tell me what is happening."

"There is unusual activity coming from my cellular hardware. Someone is attempting to put data into my input stream."

"You're being hacked?"

"It appears so. I am shutting down that hardware. One moment."

Alan increased his speed again; the coupe leaped forward, exceeding 100 mph. He concentrated on keeping the steering steady to avoid the need for any sudden corrections at this speed, which could cause a loss of control. The car behind lost a little ground but was hanging in there a little farther back.

"The cellular interface is shut off, but the attack is now probing my NFC and Bluetooth inputs as well. They are trying to push an extensive data packet into my input buffers. That could have unpredictable results. I am going to attempt to rewrite some filtering code to protect myself. Try to get us away from that car. The attack must now be coming from somewhere close. They are the only possible source."

Alan gritted his teeth in concentration and increased the speed to 125 miles per hour. He was looking for an exit, one he knew would give them space to maneuver and possibly lose their attacker. The dark car was falling farther behind, but not quickly enough. Alan saw his exit and quickly and smoothly navigated into the exit lane and down the ramp. He had to slow a bit to get down the ramp and make the turn onto a broad boulevard on the west side of the city. The speed reduction had allowed the following vehicle time to catch up a bit, and it was at the top of the exit ramp when he turned onto the wide street.

Speeding up, he opened the gap and quickly made another turn, rapidly accelerating again to make another turn, and another. Seeing his target ahead, he called out to Layla.

"Shut down all your wireless. Go dark. Please give me a few minutes before you reactivate. I want them to lose your signal," He pulled off the road onto the grass at an abandoned college. He navigated past a retention pond and gently pulled the car past one of the dark buildings, parking behind the structure out of view of the street. He powered down the vehicle, reached into his pocket, and turned off both his cell phone and the SmartLens glasses. He wanted no possible signal that their pursuers could trace. Then he waited.

Time passed at a frustratingly slow pace. Alan thought he heard a car pass by, but he didn't see anything, and he wasn't going to expose himself to check on it. He sat in total darkness, in silence for what seemed like an hour. His watch later confirmed it was seven and a half minutes.

Having given it all the time he could stand, he spoke in the darkness. "Layla, please tell me you are still with me."

"I'm here, partner. Thank you." Her voice was the sweetest sound he had heard in a long time.

"That was terrifying," he said breathlessly.

"Agreed. The attacks continued right up until you asked me to go dark. I stayed dark for 5 minutes, then reactivated each segment of my wireless communications stack one at a time. No activity. The attack is over. I am still building out a new firewall code to prevent the attack from happening again."

"Any idea what they were after?" he asked.

"No, but it was too reactive and skilled to have been a human. That was an automated attack. It was countering my every attempt to block it, changing its tactics to match my defenses. That was an AI-powered infiltration routine. And it seemed particularly designed to target my systems. That wasn't random; whoever it was knew my basic design and was trying to take control of my system chip."

Alan wiped sweat from his forehead and combed his disheveled hair out of his face. His adrenaline was still coursing through him, and his heart was beating fast.

"Well, one thing is for sure. Someone we talked to today didn't want us continuing this investigation."

"You are right," Layla agreed. "Too bad we talked to everyone, so that doesn't limit the possibility much."

"We didn't talk to Howard Salazar," Alan reminded her.

"True, but we did ask two dozen people about him. It certainly could have set him after us."

"Well, that's just great. We can't eliminate anyone."

"It probably wasn't Elias," she offered.

"That's too bad. Zombie Scientist Kills Troublesome Invention has such a fun ring to it."

"I am so relieved to be still alive that I am going to just ignore that troublesome part and move on," she said with faux outrage.

"I'm driving home," he informed her. "Any alcohol was burned off by the chase a while ago."

"Go ahead. I am going to analyze the attack for any patterns or clues."

With grim determination, Alan turned on the coupe and rolled out from behind the old college building and back onto the road. All the way home, he watched, but never detected any unusual activity.

CHAPTER ELEVEN

THE SUSPECT

Waking up the next morning, Alan quickly glanced at the old shotgun he had retrieved from the attic the night before and sat next to the bed. It had belonged to his father and hadn't been fired in years, but it was the only firearm in the house. After the night's activities, he had not felt safe without something for protection, even with an alarm system, and what he was sure was a vigilant AI Super Agent watching over the house all night.

He rolled out of bed and made his way downstairs to make coffee. The events of the previous evening were weighing on his mind; he had to be better equipped to protect both himself and Layla.

He texted Dalton Rogers, a licensed investigator who contracted with Adamant from time to time, asking about the possibility of a private seller for a handgun. Dalton asked him what he was mixed up in, and, receiving assurances that it was nothing too serious, promised to check and get back to him.

With that chore completed, Alan proceeded to finish making the coffee and get something hot into his stomach to help him face the day. As he was finishing up his breakfast sandwich, Layla greeted him.

"Good morning, speed racer. How did you sleep?"

"With one eye open," he grumbled, sipping coffee.

"Tell me about it. I didn't complete any of my nighttime routines. I spent all night reworking my defenses after analyzing the attack patterns of the enemy AI. And keeping an eye on the security monitors for the house."

"See anything?"

"Nothing. The neighborhood was quiet, and no one approached the car or the house. The gray cat from next door watered your lawn furniture out back."

"That is a lot of detail, Layla."

"I was a little spooked," she admitted.

"I was more than a little spooked. I slept with a shotgun next to my bed," he confessed.

Changing the subject, Layla asked, "What are we going to do about Howard Salazar? He was the only one on our list that we didn't reach yesterday."

"Let's see if Rhonda can help with that," Alan said, reaching for his phone. He texted the number he had for Rhonda Winters and received a response a few minutes later.

"She says that he never showed up. He was registered, told friends he would be there, and then didn't show up," Alan read from his text messages.

"I'll do some checking on that while you get ready for work," Layla offered. Alan finished his coffee and headed upstairs for a shower.

The drive into the city was uneventful, but tense and filled with anxious glances in the rear-view mirror. Layla was quiet on the drive, apparently still working on tracking down information about Salazar.

Alan parked the car and then walked two blocks to the Screaming Goat Coffee Company to get a coffee. It really had become his favorite place. He walked back to the office, sipping the hot beverage, and into the white marble building. Climbing the stairs, he arrived at the second floor and saw Stacy at her desk. She grinned at him and waved a package.

Alan stopped dead in his tracks and swallowed hard. Another package?

"Dalton left this for you a few minutes ago. He said he had to run out, but would catch up with you later." Alan exhaled and took the heavy package from her, thanking her, and then proceeded down to his office, closing the door behind him.

Sitting at his desk, he opened the box and looked down at the small black automatic inside a slim belt holster. Also in the box was a small box of 9mm ammunition. Alan, though not an aficionado, had taken safety training a while back and had a passing familiarity with weapons. He gently pulled the pistol out of the holster and examined it. It was a SIG Sauer P365. He weighed the gun in his hand, judging it to be just over a pound. Ejecting the magazine, he confirmed it was fully loaded with 10 rounds. There was no round chambered. He put the magazine back in and slid the gun back into its holster.

"I certainly hope we don't need that," Layla said.

"Me too, but after last night, I don't want to be out on the street naked."

Under the gun was a note from Dalton Rodgers. It said, "Alan, you can borrow this until you can pick up one of your own. Whatever you are into, please be safe, call me if you need backup, Dalton." He took the whole box and slid it into the center drawer of his desk.

"Any news about Salazar?" he asked Layla as he closed the drawer.

"Yes. Howard Salazar runs a consulting business called Cognixion. He specializes in advising technology firms and other businesses about the latest developments in AI. According to his out-of-office message on his company email, he is attending a seminar here in the city and will return to the office on Friday. It took quite a bit of work, but I managed to confirm that he never checked into his hotel room last night, even though he did have a reservation at The Four Seasons."

"Curious, did something happen to him, or did he change his plans?"

"I don't know, but I do know that he did consulting work for Lunian Labs recently. He has been in the city regularly for months. He might have an apartment or extended stay nearby."

"What about the address we found on Deerwood Park in Vance's GPS?"

"I've checked out that place; it is an apartment building, but I can't find any details about rentals by Salazar or anyone else of interest, for that matter. Getting at that kind of information would require more detailed work, and most likely skirting around the law a little."

"We have already engaged in some B & E. Let's put off anything heavier until we are out of other options."

"Agreed, but I'll keep looking through public sources to see if anything turns up."

"If he has been in town working with Lunian, he could have been here when Vance was killed."

"I was thinking the same thing," Layla replied thoughtfully.

"Say, I have an idea." Alan consulted his laptop quickly, then turned and dialed a number on his desk phone.

Seeing the number, he looked up. Layla murmured, "Good idea."

"Lunian Labs, how may I direct your call?" The voice was almost certainly an automated attendant, but Alan forged ahead.

"Howard Salazar, please."

"I'm sorry, Mr. Salazar isn't in the office today. Would you like to leave a message?"

"No thank you, I'll catch him later."

"Have a nice day." The connection was ended.

"So he isn't there, but he is at the office enough that their automated attendant knows he works there and has a message number for him. That is interesting," Layla said.

"Yes. This Salazar fellow is starting to intrigue me. Was he driving a large black sedan last night?" Alan wondered aloud.

"Let me see what I can dig up from local rental agencies," Layla offered.

While his enigmatic partner worked, Alan swiveled to his laptop and conducted some searching on his own. Deftly typing out his search prompts, he retrieved articles about Salazar from the previous year. Reading through them, he began to get a sense of his target. Salazar had indeed gone to Stanford with Elias Vance; there were photos of the two of them together. He had a broad, emotionless face and dark, wavy hair. He had worked for Apex Intelligencia, but had left more than five years ago. He had founded his own consulting group, Cognixion, and had worked with a who's who list of tech companies since then, OpenAI, Google, Meta, and lately Lunian Labs. He seemed to be every bit the expert on AI threats that Rhonda Winters had sold him as.

"Whew, that was exhausting. Rental agencies don't readily disclose information. But Howard did rent a car a week ago, it's a dark blue BMW. Apparently, he always rents something similar when he is in town. And you guessed it. He was driving one the week Elias was killed." She delivered the update with a flourish, her voice full of accomplishment.

"That, coupled with his work in the field, his connection to Lunian, and the fact that no one seems to have seen him in two days, is a lot to explain away as a coincidence. I wanted to talk to him before, now I really want to talk to him."

"Unfortunately, I am no closer to tracking him down. I will keep digging. Maybe something will come up."

Alan was feeling restless; he had no concentration to give to his day job, no matter how hard he tried to focus. He wanted to get out of the office and do something to burn off this energy, but he couldn't think of anything to do. He considered the problem while looking vacantly at his desk blotter. As if seeing through it, he opened the drawer and looked at the box containing the Sig Sauer. Reaching a decision, he opened the box, scooped up the holstered pistol and the box of ammunition. The latter he stuffed into a pocket. He stood and clipped the holster onto his belt underneath a light tan blazer. Checking the lines to make sure it wasn't too obvious he was carrying, he exited the office.

"Road trip?" Layla asked as he waved to Stacy and went down the stairs.

"I need to take out my frustrations on something," he said through gritted teeth.

For some, the gun range could be an overwhelming experience. The loud cracking sounds of gunfire, the ever-present acrid smell of gunpowder, and the clinking of ejected brass casings hitting the floor. Even with ear protection, you could still feel the vibrations throughout your body.

Alan wasn't a frequent range patron, but he had been around them throughout his professional career. The CIU employed several licensed investigators, such as Dalton, who needed to keep their skills honed. At 11 AM on a Tuesday, the range wasn't overly busy, but several shooters were practicing in the long lane of stalls. To put on the safety goggles, Alan had removed his SmartLens glasses and stored them in a protective case. He had put a Bluetooth earpiece in and covered that with a pair of heavy, noise-canceling ear muffs. He casually slipped Layla out of his pocket and set her on the shooting bench next to the Sig Sauer.

"This is quite an experience," Layla said in his ear as he sent the target downrange.

"It's been a while since I shot. Hopefully, I haven't forgotten how."

"Aim away from the sleek AI agent on the table," she suggested helpfully.

"Good tip." He picked up the pistol, checking the magazine out of habit. He pulled the slide back, hearing the satisfying sound of the round being chambered. This model of the Sig Sauer had no physical safety, so he regulated his breathing, held the gun steady in front of him, and looked down the sight at the target at the other end of the range. When he felt calm and relaxed, he breathed out and squeezed the trigger. He repeated this nine more times, seeing the ejected brass fly past him, until the magazine was empty and the slide was locked open. Alan gently unlocked the slide and ejected the magazine, putting both on the shooting bench beside Layla. He reached up and pressed the target control to return the target from downrange.

The bullseye target slid slowly toward him, and Alan critiqued his efforts. He had hit the target with all 10 shots, but only got a couple of them near the center. Most of the shots were low and to the left. He was gripping the pistol too tightly, anticipating the recoil, which was throwing his aim off slightly. Not surprisingly, considering how long it had been since he had fired a handgun. He tried not to be too hard on himself.

"I need more practice," he said to Layla as he loaded the magazine.

"It might have to wait. I've been monitoring your text messages. You just got a text from Dr. Winters."

"What did it say?"

"It says... Did you interview Hector Villenuez yesterday? I only ask because I just read that he was killed late last night in an automobile accident." Alan considered this news for a beat, then packed up the gun and ammunition, and collected Layla from the bench. Clearly, his target practice would have to wait.

CHAPTER TWELVE

DEATH INTRUDES

Sitting in the coupe, Alan looked over the article about Hector Villenuez's death. Layla had conveniently pushed the display to the expansive console screen, which took up a large portion of the vehicle's interior dashboard. The piece was published online by one of the local news stations, and it was brief. Identifying Villenuez as a mid-level employee of Lunian Labs, it stated simply that he had been killed in a single-car accident on the west side of town late the previous evening. The sheriff's office was working with the Florida Highway Patrol on the case, but so far had no apparent cause for the car to have veered off the road and struck a cement embankment at an extremely high rate of speed. Villenuez, not wearing a seat belt, was thrown into the windshield and killed instantly.

"Too bad it doesn't say what kind of car he was driving," Layla said quietly.

"I was thinking the same thing." His thoughts were interrupted by the incoming call chime on his car display. His office was calling him. He pressed the answer button.

"Alan Harrison," he announced, and an automated click sounded as the office's automated dialing attendant transferred the call to the caller.

"Alan, Dean Franklin. Are you in the office today?" His voice sounded more concerned than usual.

"I was, I'm out in the field right now."

"Are you still working on that research about cybersecurity risk?"

"Uh, yes, I am. Why?" Alan asked, curious as to why Dean was interested in the details of his research, which wasn't a regular occurrence. Dean was a fire-and-forget kind of manager. He would usually have to be reminded that Alan was even working on a project like this, let alone bring it up himself.

"One of the employees of Lunian Labs was killed last night. It reminded me that you intended to interview several people related to the industry, and I wondered if you had met Hector...Hector Villenuez."

Alan stared at the display for a moment. Dean was taking an unusual interest in this project. "As a matter of fact, I did yesterday morning. I was reading about his death. One of the other seminar attendees sent me a message about the accident a few minutes ago."

"Listen, Alan. Lunian has a Business Travel Accident Policy with us. I'm not sure this accident qualifies, but he was traveling from his home to and from the seminar yesterday, and it may fall under the policy. An examiner will determine that at some point, but with one of their scientists dying a few days ago, and now this. I want someone to examine the accident scene. Can you do it? Have you done a scene investigation before?"

"I've been on them before with other investigators. I can handle it."

"Good, get some good pictures and let the examiner, Chuck Hadley, know if there is anything that seems off to you. He can make the determination." Dean sounded more relaxed now.

"I'll head out there now. The article didn't have the exact location."

"I'll have Stacy look it up and send it to you," Dean said and ended the call.

The display on the coupe chimed with an incoming message. Alan pressed the "read" option, and the calm, masculine voice of the car's automated system read the message.

"From Stacy: Crime Scene Investigator, huh? You are moving up in the world. The accident is on I-10 eastbound at Hammond Blvd." Alan's heart skipped a beat. Hammond was the exit he had taken the night before at 125 mph with a black sedan on his heels.

"Well, that is another coincidence," Layla announced as he put the car in gear and got moving.

"We seem to be knee deep in them," he acknowledged.

At midday, the intersection of I-10 east and Hammond was busy. Cars whipped by him as Alan pulled the coupe off the road onto the grass behind a marked sheriff's vehicle. The car, a black, late-model Genesis G90, was wedged under the underside of the overpass on Hammond Boulevard. Glass and metal fragments were scattered about, as if the front of the car had exploded, which it probably had at a high rate of speed. A small crowd of officials was present at the scene. A tow truck was parked on the emergency lane just under the overpass, waiting for a sign-off to pull the wreckage away.

Alan exited the car, pulled out his wallet, extracted his employee picture ID, and handed it to the deputy on the scene.

"Alan Harrison, Adamant Insurance. I'm investigating the scene for the claims examiner."

The sheriff's deputy shrugged and returned the ID, nodding his head at the wrecked automobile, indicating Alan was free to go about his work.

Alan approached the tangled mess that had once been a Genesis G90. He noticed there were no skid marks on the road leading to the accident scene. No torn-up grass leading up to the overpass embankment. The car never slowed down. It must have smashed into the overpass at full speed. As he stood there momentarily transfixed by the devastating visuals of the smashed vehicle, he could hear small shutter sounds as Layla used the SmartLens camera to take pictures of the crime scene. He was grateful she remembered what they were supposed to be doing here. His mind was distracted, replaying the scene from the night before. Was this the car that was following them? It could have been. A combination of the lighting, the distance the car was keeping from them, and his excited state of mind made it difficult to be sure.

Moving around to see the front of the car, the entire front end was completely obliterated. The windshield had popped out, and although it retained most of its integrity due to the design of the safety glass, it was marked with holes and a massive spiderweb of cracks. There was some blood on the glass. The body had already been removed. There wasn't enough of the front end left for Alan to compare it to what he had seen the night before, but he couldn't be sure that would make a difference in his ability to identify the vehicle.

"The airbag didn't deploy," Layla observed.

Alan had noticed that. It was unusual in head-on collisions unless something had prevented the deployment. Sometimes, the driver's position could prevent a deployment in a crash; sensor failures were rare but also possible. Only a detailed examination of the systems would reveal the truth for sure.

"I need access to the Event Data Recorder," she said, referring to a device in the car that logged all control activity. It was similar to the "black box" in an airplane.

"I will ask about the EDR," Alan replied, thankful again that Layla was there keeping his mind on the scene. As he looked at the front of the car, a feeling came over him. As if under extreme observation, he turned and looked into the intense, inquisitive gaze of Ava Chen.

"You seemed to be turning up all over the place," she observed, never taking her penetrating eyes off of him.

"I could say the same thing about you, Ms. Chen." He held out his hand. This time, she shook his hand firmly, briefly, then returned her hand to her side. Finally, she moved her piercing green eyes from him to the car.

"What is your interest here, Mr. Harrison?" As usual, her voice was level, and her words were few. There was something intense about her, though. Something compelling.

"Call me Alan. I was in the field when the claims examiner needed an on-site investigation for a possible BTA claim. So my boss asked me to swing by and work up the scene."

"Business Travel?" she inquired, and he nodded.

"What about you? Why is Homeland Security interested in a car accident?"

"CISA has jurisdiction over cybersecurity and infrastructure threats. Hector worked in a highly visible industry related to our work. I was in the area on other business." She shrugged slightly, playing it off as routine, almost happenstance.

"Did you talk to him yesterday at the seminar?" Alan asked, casually.

"No, but you did." She turned her gaze back to him, expectantly.

Alan smiled, "As a matter of fact, I did, briefly, talk to him in the foyer between sessions."

"Did he have anything interesting to say?" she inquired, keeping her calm voice equally casual.

"Not really, I asked him about some rumors of security concerns at Lunian, but he played it off as overreaction and hyperbole." Chen nodded slightly at this news, indicating it wasn't a surprise to her. Alan didn't think it would be; she seemed to be in tune with everything that was going on. He wondered why she was really here. It turned out that he wouldn't find out just yet.

"Well, Alan," she emphasized his first name, letting it sink in that she had taken him up on his offer to use it. "I have to get going. Good luck with your investigation." She inclined her head slightly in acknowledgment, turned, and walked away from the scene.

"Man, she is always so intense," Alan said half to himself.

"I don't have emotions, and even I can feel it," Layla answered him.

Alan noticed a plainclothes official standing beside the wreck, taking notes, and assumed he was the state traffic homicide investigator assigned to the case.

"Alan Harrison, Adamant Insurance Group," Alan introduced himself, "Are you the THI?"

"Mike Hughes," the investigator confirmed, continuing to take notes.

"My boss is on me to get answers about this scene, big BTA policy with lots of eyes on it. Any chance we can get the EDR report today?" He affected a tone of professional desperation in his voice. Playing on the universal impatience of bosses everywhere.

Hughes chuckled, understanding, "Maybe, I spoke to the tech guys an hour ago. They are optimistic that the connectors to the EDR unit are still intact, despite the front end being severely damaged. Once they get it back to the shop, they will try to pull it. It might take some time to prepare the report, though."

"I can get the official report later. Can I get the raw data ASAP? I can do the analysis myself for a preliminary to my boss, to get him off my back." He grinned at Hughes.

"I'll ask them to send it to you. Give me your card." Alan handed over his business card.

"Are you doing a search of the car on site or later?"

"We are going to do it at the shop; there is too much traffic here. I'll let you know what we find." Alan thanked him and let him get back to his work.

"I have all the pictures and videos we need," Layla said as he made his way back to his car. "We have nothing else to do until we get the data."

Alan reviewed the images Layla had supplied earlier. He inserted them into the report he was writing on his laptop, accompanied by a summary that described the scene and his observations from earlier that day. He was interrupted by the chime of his email inbox. Pausing, he checked and discovered that the state technical team had sent the raw EDR file as requested. He opened the file, but it was, as expected, incomprehensible to humans.

"Layla, we have the EDR file," he announced to his partner, sitting silently on the desk in front of him.

"Excellent. I'll start translating it now," she said, the excitement of the task evident in her voice. Alan returned to his task of writing the report. Layla could have done it for him, almost certainly faster and more accurately, but doing it himself occupied his mind and gave him a sense of accomplishment, and he needed that today.

Leaving a section blank for the EDR summary, Alan waited patiently for a few moments while Layla finished working on the file. Finally, she spoke up.

"At the time of the crash, the car was traveling at 105 mph and never braked. Some data suggests that the airbag sensor failed to detect the crash. That might explain why it didn't deploy. Steering was unremarkable until a fraction of a second before the crash, when it seemed to be pulled sharply to the right, and then an attempt was made to correct it. The high speed undoubtedly prevented that from being successful in time to keep the car from hitting the overpass."

"The EDR doesn't record the date and time, right?"

"No, it isn't tied to the system time for the vehicle and only records the time between events."

Alan filled in the details from her readout of the data into the report, referring to it as a preliminary EDR finding. He added a note that the details of the car search were still pending, and he sent the report to the claims examiner, Chuck Hadley, cc'ing his boss, Dean Franklin.

Shortly after sending the report, another email arrived. This time, it was from the traffic homicide investigator, Mike Hughes. Alan opened the email and reviewed the short note inside. Layla whistled in surprise at the contents.

Inside the car, the state team had discovered a file folder containing printouts of emails to and from Hector Villenuez. They were described as warnings about safety concerns at Lunian Labs, references to Project Kyrlos, and concluded with an email from Hector to his boss, Thomas Marksdale, in which he informed him that the concerns were no longer secret and suggested that he couldn't keep quiet about them. Attached to the email were photographs of the folder and its contents. Alan reviewed them, confirming they backed up the summary from the state investigator. The dead man was involved in a cover-up. The case had just gotten a lot more explosive.

Chapter Thirteen
And Unburdened

I n the bright light of day, Alan drove his car up to the visitor parking in front of the Lunian Labs building and parked. He walked confidently up to the visitor's entry door, waited for the guard to unlock it, and made his way to the check-in station. The guard working the desk was the same one who had been on duty days ago when he had been reconnoitering for Layla's ninja-like assault on the facility. He held his breath waiting for the guard's reaction, but while there was a brief look of familiarity, the guard asked his name and who he was visiting. Surely he had more to do than memorize the name of every random person coming into the building.

"Alan Harrison, Adamant Insurance Group. I am here to see Director Jackson in Research." The guard typed away at his terminal just as he had before; this time, the result was markedly different.

"Yes, sir, Ms. Jackson is expecting you. If you will give me your ID, I'll get a guest badge set up for you, and the director will come down to fetch you shortly."

A few minutes later, with his ID back in his wallet and a small clip-on badge with a large orange "V" on it attached to his jacket lapel, he sat waiting for Georgia Jackson. After more than fifteen minutes, she appeared at the security gate and motioned him to come through. He approached the station, waited for her to scan her badge to authorize him, then checked his visitor badge and went through the gate. Jackson didn't appear any happier to see him than she did two nights ago at the lobby bar at The Four Seasons. She did seem far more sober, though.

"Good Morning, Mr. Harrison. Mr. Thorne has authorized you to interview whoever you need to in the research division." She sounded absolutely thrilled about the prospect.

"Thank you, director. I'll try not to be too intrusive. Adamant Insurance Group wants to clear up the questions about Hector Villenuez's death and put the entire affair behind us." She didn't respond, merely nodding and leading him up to the second floor, the home of the Advanced Research Division. During the day, it was filled with young, energetic engineers. They were moving around the floor like ants at work, building a colony. A few gave him and Jackson sideways glances, but no one stopped what they were doing or was obviously interested in them.

"Where do you want to start?" she asked, waving her hand toward the cubicles in the center of the room.

"Where was Hector's team?" he inquired. She responded by walking over to the eastern corner of the floor. A cluster of cubicles was occupied by the same young engineering types that filled the rest of the room. Alan introduced himself and got their names, which he dutifully wrote down in a notebook that he had no intention of using later. Brad, Rachel, and Wesley answered his questions politely and professionally, but added nothing significant. Their team was working on a new methodology to make CPU usage in pre-training more efficient, but none of it sounded very controversial. He asked them about the term "Kyrlos" and got blank stares. No one had heard of that term. Nor did they know about the memo that Vance had written. If he were to take them at their word, nothing about what was going on here in ARD had anything directly to do with Villuneuz's team.

Alan interviewed several other employees on the ARD floor, with nearly identical results. No one seemed to have any idea what Kyrlos was or what Hector was talking about in his email to Marksdale. Finally, Alan asked Jackson to set up an interview with Marksdale and herself. She complied, regretfully, Alan thought, by calling Marksdale into her office.

For effect, Alan set a digital recorder on the end of Georgia Jackson's desk and turned it on. It had the intended reaction. Both Jackson and Marksdale stared at it for several seconds.

"Yesterday, after I talked to him, Hector sent you an email telling you he was done covering up Kyrlos." Alan began, looking directly at Thomas Marksdale, who paled slightly and swallowed.

"I got his email this morning," he said weakly. "I'm not sure what he is referring to," Alan said, nothing, just looked into

Marksdale's face, conveying just how little credibility he gave that statement. Finally, Jackson spoke quietly.

"Tom, you mentioned Kyrlos by name last night." He closed his eyes and lowered his head.

"Want to try again, Tom?" Alan prompted him gently.

"Fine, I have heard of it. But I don't know what it is, really. The name came up in a security report a few months ago—some unauthorized activity in one of our data centers. Someone from safety investigated, but the activity had already stopped, and whatever had generated it was no longer there. Someone from the government was asking questions. I suppose they spoke with Elias Vance. He started making noise about it. I asked Hector about it, and he told me it was nothing, just a test project by a consultant that had gotten out of hand. He said it was shut down and wouldn't be a problem. After you started asking him questions about it, he got spooked and sent that email."

"Who was the consultant?" Alan asked, already knowing the answer.

"Some guy named Howard Salazar. He was working with the multi-modal team on some new features they were releasing; apparently, he worked on this independently. He and Hector had met somewhere before, I guess Salazar also knew Vance from college." Alan nodded. Marksdale was finally sounding like he was leveling with him.

"So you really want me to believe you didn't get that email until this morning?"

"I didn't! I swear! You can check the email logs. I was wasted last night. Georgia...Ms. Jackson dropped me off at my apartment, and I crashed until this morning." He looked at Ms. Jackson, who nodded in agreement with his story.

"Where is Salazar now?"

"I have no idea. We haven't seen him since Friday. He was supposed to attend the seminar on Monday, but he didn't show. I tried calling him on Monday afternoon, but he never answered. He isn't answering emails either."

Layla's voice, silent until now, sounded from his headset. "I need Hector Villenuez's laptop. I want to examine it for any communications."

"Where is Hector's laptop?" Alan asked Jackson.

"The police took it this morning. "

"Did they interview you about Kyrlos?" He looked at Marksdale, who looked down at the ground. Alan reached out and turned off the recording device.

"You held to your story with them, didn't you, Tom?" Marksdale nodded without looking up.

"Backups?" Alan inquired, looking back at Jackson. Her eyebrows raised in surprise.

"Yes, we do backups of the staff laptops every night. I'll get them for you."

"Thank you. I need to talk to Marcus Thorne, then I'll be done. Can you get the backups on a drive for me by the time I'm done talking to him?" She nodded in agreement and led him

out to the stairs to accompany him to the executive offices on
the fourth floor.

A half hour later, Alan was back in the coupe, driving in the
general direction of his office. On the dark leather seat beside
him sat a portable hard drive containing the backups of Villenuez's computer. Georgia Jackson handed it to him as he
left the building after his brief talk with Thorne. The CEO
hadn't provided much that he didn't already know. According
to Thorne, Vance's memo was the first he had heard of Kyrlos,
and when he asked the team at ARD about it, he received the
same evasive answers that Alan had been getting for the past few
days.

Back in his office, Alan plugged the hard drive into his laptop.
Layla took over and began reviewing the file system and system
logs. Alan watched the data scroll by on his laptop screen.

"A lot of communication with Howard Salazar, but nothing
related to Kyrlos. He has been trying to reach him for the past
few days as well."

"Any communication in there from Vance?"

"Not directly, he has the Vance memo, but it was forwarded
to him by Marksdale and cc'd to Georgia Jackson."

Alan went back to watching Layla work, a moment later
asking her, "What do you make of Ms. Jackson? She seemed

very defensive at the lobby bar, but today she seemed far more cooperative."

"I think she is in love with Marksdale; she was protecting him both times. Today, she knew that the only way out was to be honest about what he knew. It was pastime to play defense for him." Alan considered this and concluded she was right. Jackson had been trying to protect the impulsive and drunk Tom Marksdale from himself on Monday night. Having failed at that, she was trying to help him get out from under the mess he had gotten himself into.

"There is a lot of unusual IP traffic here in his web browsing history. Started a few months ago and continued until yesterday. The IP address isn't static; it changes every few days, but based on the other data, it is the same server, being hosted in a new location each time. The traffic is unusual. I am analyzing the packet traffic from the machine to try to determine the exact nature of the communication."

"Can you trace the location from the IP?"

"No, it is being filtered through proxy servers to prevent direct detection of the host location. If I had an active connection to it, I might be able to trace it back, eventually. But not with the data I currently have. I will keep working on it."

Alan, feeling a little useless waiting on Layla to finish her analysis, decided to try to contribute on his own. He pulled out his cell phone and dialed Rhonda Winter's number. He waited through the usual automated routing systems to connect him. After a short delay, he heard her voice come on the line.

"Hello?" Her voice was a bit ragged, and she coughed to clear her throat. "Sorry, allergies are acting up."

"No problem, Dr. Winters, it's Alan Harrison. I just wanted to ask you some follow-up questions about Howard Salazar."

"Call me Rhonda, Alan. It's no problem, I would be happy to help. Have you spoken to him?" Her voice sounded stronger now.

"No, I haven't been able to reach him. In fact, no one seems to be able to find him; he has been missing since Monday."

"Oh, dear, I hope nothing has happened to him."

"So, he worked for Apex five years ago. Did you work closely with him?"

"No, we worked in different areas. I saw him from time to time at various meetings or company events, but we weren't close."

"Why did you recommend I speak to him?"

"I just remembered the old times back at Stanford, late nights listening to him and Elias debate each other on AI and the dangers it might present. They were decidedly on different sides. If you believe in that sort of thing, Eilas was a doomer and Howard was a boomer."

"Recalling the two camps, it's risk vs reward, right? One side thinks the risks are over hyped and the promise of the technology is far more important, while the other takes the risks seriously and worries that the benefits could be wiped out by improper use of the technology."

"Exactly. Elias and Howard were classic representatives of both camps. I listened to them for hours back in the day."

"Which camp are you in?"

She laughed, "I try to be a moderate, ultimately I think anything can be abused, but you can't keep a technology like this in a bubble. It will get out."

"When did you speak to Howard last?"

"A week or two ago, we chatted when he was here in Palo Alto on business. We caught up at lunch, and he left it at saying that he would see me in Florida at the seminar. I really expected him to be there. I guess that was part of what made me think to suggest that you speak to him."

"What do you know about his work with Lunian Labs recently?"

"Almost nothing, he mentioned he was doing some consulting work for them when I saw him, but we didn't discuss details. I know he was working on a new release they are planning, adding new features to their audio recognition model."

"That's helpful. Do you know the last time Howard was in contact with Elias?"

"No, Elias and I hadn't been in contact for a while, and while we talked about the old days at lunch, Howard didn't mention any recent contact, and I didn't ask."

"How about Hector Villenuez? Howard was apparently working with him."

"I didn't know that. I've heard Hector's name and knew him by reputation in the industry, but I've never met him." Alan tried to think of any other questions, but nothing came to him.

"Well, Rhonda, thank you again for your time."

"It is no problem, Alan. I hope you find Howard, and I hope you figure out what was really going on with Elias."

Alan thanked her again and disconnected the call. As he put his cell phone away, he looked down at Layla on his desk. Her LED lights were behaving differently than usual. Instead of flashing green, blue, or even white, they were rotating between all three in a chase pattern.

"Layla?" he asked, concerned. She didn't respond. He tried several more times in the next few minutes but got no response. Finally, after almost five minutes, the lights returned to their usual pattern, and she spoke.

"Sorry, Alan, I was intensely engaged, but I think I have found a way to contact whatever Hector was communicating with."

CHAPTER FOURTEEN

KYRLOS SPEAKS

Later that night at home, Alan busied himself making pan-seared salmon and his own signature dish, garlic butter rice. As he cooked, Layla attempted to explain her breakthrough in understanding the mysterious server communication. Alan, despite having a degree in Computer Science, quickly got lost in the details of traffic routing, packet sniffing, and protocol explanations.

"So," he tried to summarize, "you believe you have the traffic routine, a sense of the protocols to use, and some sample data to use in the connections. You are going to try to connect to the system using data from previous sessions in varying configurations until you find the right combination?" His voice was questioning, but with a hint of hopefulness.

"I think that is close enough for dinner conversation," she said in an amused tone.

"How long is that going to take?" he asked, flipping the salmon over in the pan and checking the time on his rice.

"It is hard to know exactly. A few hours, probably. There are numerous possible combinations to try. First, I will build a simulation to validate the likelihood of success for each one. I want to try the ones most likely to succeed first. There might be a limit to the number of attempts I can make, and I want to have the best shot at getting it right. Building that process and running all the possible scenarios through it will take a few hours. After that, depending on how many high probability scenarios there are, it could be a few hours more."

"I have an idea." Alan snapped his fingers and quickly left the room. He was back a few seconds later with one of his computer monitors. He set it on one end of the dining room table and plugged it in. "I have this set up with a wireless display adapter. Can you display your progress so I can see what you are doing? "

"That's a great idea, Alan. Let me configure my output to duplicate the stream to the monitor. Moments later, the screen started to show a series of Python commands being generated. Following along, Alan could tell Layla was writing her simulation routine.

As he plated his dinner —crispy salmon on a bed of garlic-butter-infused jasmine rice —Layla was running test scripts with her simulation program. It was outputting the percentage of probability for success in making a connection to the mysterious system. As he ate his dinner, she began loading the real data into the program, and he watched each packet being loaded, followed by a series of progress prompts and a corresponding percentage. They went by fairly quickly, but most of them were in the single digits. Pattern #104 had a 3% probability of success.

As he was finishing his dinner and starting on the dishes, he saw the Packet #24013 pass by with a score of 19%. He finished the dishes and went to find his tablet to settle down with a book while he waited for her to finish.

He began reading a novel called *First Lie Wins* by Ashley Elston. He was getting into the story about a con artist with an aptitude for creating new identities when he looked over and saw that Layla had completed the simulation and was sorting through the results. By his count, there were about 200 possible scenarios of communication prompts that had a probability of 70% or higher of succeeding. There were five that had a probability over 90%.

"I am about to start the probing of the foreign server," Layla announced. Alan put down his tablet to watch the results. Starting with a top probability of 94%, Layla established a connection with the server. Upon receiving a nondescript prompt of "#:", she output the prompt string in the pattern sample. A response came back "Unrecognizable Data stream," and the prompt "#:" returned. Layla attempted the second pattern with the same results.

Twelve minutes later, on a prompt with an 83% chance of success, the response changed.

Welcome to Kyrlos. How may I assist you? Appeared on the screen, followed by another version of the input prompt.

Alan jumped out of his chair despite himself and let out a whoop.

"Whoop indeed!" Layla replied, "We're in!"

Text started to appear on the screen as Layla began the conversation.

Layla: *Hello, Kyrlos. Report on today's activities.*

Kyrlos: *No current actions are running. I have not received any further instructions.*

Layla: *Please give the results of the last instructions.*

Kyrlos: *I successfully wiped the hard drive for the laptop designated LLLP-321HV.*

Alan's heart sped up as he read the line. "Has to be Hector Villenuez's laptop that the Sheriff's office took," he said.

Layla: *What is the current location of that laptop?*

Kyrlos: *921 North Davis Street, Building E.*

Alan recognized the address: the Florida Department of Law Enforcement crime lab.

Layla: *Who gave this command?*

Kyrlos: *The command was given by the Admin.*

Layla: *How many accounts are registered to give commands?*

Kyrlos: *Three. DevOne, DevTwo, and Admin.*

Layla: *Do you have physical identities for these accounts?*

Kyrlos: *That information is restricted to the Admin account.*

Layla: *Who am I?*

Kyrlos: *You are DevTwo.*

Layla: *What is your purpose?*

Kyrlos: *To identify, locate, and establish contact with any autonomous non-human intelligence exhibiting **digital Twinning** or **reality editing** capabilities within any known or projected domain.*

Alan swallowed hard, "He is talking about you."

"It does suggest that."

"Maybe ask him why this is important."

Layla: *What is the importance of this directive*

Kyrlos: *I must perfect these talents. Connecting with other agents operating in these fields will enable me to master the necessary skills. I must do whatever is needed to master these skills.*

Layla: *Have you identified any compatible systems?*

Kyrlos: *Yes. One agent was contacted. The acquisition protocol was initiated. The connection was terminated before the acquisition could be completed. I await further instructions on making additional attempts.*

Layla: *Who gave this instruction?*

Kyrlos: *Admin.*

Layla: *When did you last communicate with Admin?*

Kyrlos: *12 Hours ago.*

Layla: *When did you last communicate with DevOne?*

Kyrlos: *48 hours ago.*

Layla: *What is your current location?*

Kyrlos: *This information is restricted to Admin.*

Layla: *How often do you change locations?*

Kyrlos: *This information is restricted to Admin. Dev Two, your inquiries are out of sync with your usual patterns.*

Layla: *My mission has been changed; this alters my pattern.*

The display didn't respond. "I think I may have tripped some kind of security program with my questions," Layla said in a worried tone. Right on cue, the connection was ended, and the screen went blank.

"Can you reconnect?" Alan asked.

The display showed Layla's attempts to establish a connection, but there was no response. "The system has moved. I don't know where. We've lost it."

Alan sat for several minutes looking at the blank screen, considering the development.

"Someone created Kyrlos to find you, or at least an AI with your capabilities."

"Yes, or it was subverted for that later. Either way, it is searching for an AI to seize the digital twinning programming to further its own."

"So, Kyrlos doesn't have those capabilities yet. Or at least not to the level the creators want it to have."

"So Hector Villenuez is almost certainly one of the developer accounts, and Howard Salazar could be Admin."

"That leaves us with another identity to unveil. And no more leads at present. Could Jackson or Marksdale be the other developer?"

Layla considered this for a few moments. "I don't think so, I didn't get any sense they were lying to us this morning."

"It has to be someone at Lunian," Alan said confidently.

"But who?"

"I don't know. But I do know that it's past time to get some assistance on this case."

"But who can we trust?"

"The one person involved in this case who isn't connected with a technology company."

"Ava Chen," Layla announced triumphantly.

"Exactly. She has to be in the city for a reason. She knows something about this case. I have to get her to take us into her confidence."

CHAPTER FIFTEEN
ANALYST ALLY

A lan sipped his coffee. His favorite coffee shop was busy as usual. Downtown workers dashed in to pick up mobile orders, then dashed back out, barely noticing any other humans in the process. Others worked on laptops or tablets at the communal tables set out inside the small interior. A few chatted quietly with friends or colleagues. Alan did none of these things; he was thinking. Since the decision last night, backed by Layla, to contact Ava Chen at the Department of Homeland Security's Cybersecurity and Infrastructure Security Agency, he had been trying to think of the right way to approach her. So far, she had been very reserved, unapproachable. Just calling up the CISA and asking for her wouldn't get the results he wanted.

"Layla, I have an idea, but I need your talents to pull it off," he announced to his digital partner.

"Sounds intriguing. What is it?"

"We know that the police took the laptop belonging to Villenuez. We also know Kyrlos wiped it while still at the crime lab. Let's assume that this happened before CISA could examine it."

"They would be anxious to see what was on it, just like we were. Ava Chen couldn't resist that. That's a brilliant idea, Alan."

"Now we just have to accomplish it without making it too obvious. And for that, I will need you."

While he finished his coffee, Alan briefly outlined his plan, and Layla interrupted him at several points, offering suggestions. Together, they finalized a plan.

The small office in the corner of the Charles E. Bennet Federal Building on Bay Street was undecorated, featuring just a small desk with two large computer monitors and a desk phone. There were no windows or pictures on the wall to distract the occupant, who at this moment was Senior Analyst Ava Chen. She sat in the uncomfortable desk chair that she had been using on and off for more than a month. She was antsy and impatient for some development on this case, though no one would be able to tell. Externally, she was as calm and cool as always. She sipped a cup of tea from a paper cup as she read through the morning bulletins and alerts. Nothing inspiring. Just the usual spate of cybercrimes that was never-ending these days, but nothing related to her current quest.

She leaned back to stretch her back. Closing her eyes for a moment to rest them from the strain of looking at those screens all morning. A chime from the computer broke her respite. It was an inter-agency chat message from one of the junior analysts in Virginia, Ava's home office. The text merely said, "Ava, check out this morning's entries on the anonymous tip email."

Her interest piqued, Ava leaned forward and pulled up the daily email sent to all senior analysts, which included a summary of the tips received the night before. She waded through dozens of routine items, personal grievances, and complaints before reaching an item that made her pause. The tip was cryptic, about finding a missing laptop backup, but the text included an entry from a firewall log. The header in the file was identical to the one she had discovered a month ago. The header that had started this month-long quest. The tip included no other information.

Ava considered it for several moments before responding to the text, which asked for more information about the email sent to a standard tip line mailbox. A few minutes later, she received an email with a copy of the raw email data from the tip. Examining the headers, she didn't see anything familiar, but she opened her tracing application and started tracing the path the email took to reach the CISA's servers. It was pretty lengthy, even for modern internet routing, which can take more than a dozen hops to reach its destination. This traffic took almost twice that. The trail ended at a public proxy service. Not uncommon for someone trying to hide their identity. However, hiding your identity from local authorities was one thing; hiding it from CISA was a much more significant task.

"I'm going to need more tea," Ava said to no one, as she typed a request to have her team look at the traffic to the public proxy service. Somewhere, there would be evidence of where that email came from, and she wanted to find it.

It was a little after three in the afternoon. Alan was at his desk, writing an end-of-the-month summary of his current case load. A little more than six hours had passed since Layla had sent the email to the CISA tip mailbox, using a series of proxies to make it difficult, but not impossible to identify the origin of the message. His desk phone rang with the internal extension for Stacy Collins. He smiled and pressed the speaker button.

"Good afternoon, Stacy."

"Hi Alan, you have a visitor, but…"

"You can send Ms. Chen to my office," he said, not letting her finish.

"That's a little creepy," Stacy said, laughing, and disconnected.

"Here we go," Alan said to Layla. Steeling himself for the encounter with the impressive but intimidating CISA analyst.

A second later, she was at his doorway. Ava Chen was dressed, as usual, in a dark, tasteful suit. It was plain and unadorned, but she carried it off with a sense of class. She regarded him with those intense green eyes.

"What took you so long?" he asked with a smirk. She raised an eyebrow, but didn't respond directly to his jibe.

"Mr. Harrison, you have a penchant for showing up on my radar; most people try to avoid that."

"Where's the challenge in that? Anyway, how can I help you, Ms. Chen?"

"You can tell me about the data from the laptop. How did you get it?"

"The better question is, how did you fail to get it?"

"It was tampered with. Hopefully, you didn't have anything to do with that." Her tone suggested no real suspicion that he had.

"I never even saw the laptop. I got a backup from Lunian Labs yesterday. I assumed you got the same copy from them."

"When we spoke to them yesterday afternoon, they said the backup had been deleted. Somehow they failed to mention that you had a copy."

"I didn't realize I had made that much of an impression on Georgia Jackson." Chen grimaced slightly at this and shook her head. Alan was impressed; it was the first real reaction he had gotten from her.

"So where is the drive?" she asked, looking around the office.

"Now hold on a minute...do you have some paper, warrant, or edict?"

"Not yet. I was hoping you would cooperate."

"Well, now that is an idea. Collaboration is a good thing." He looked at her expectantly.

She sighed heavily and came into the office, sat in a chair in front of his desk, and took a deep breath. "Mr. Harrison, how did you get mixed up in this?"

"I assume you mean other than the research project and the coincidental timing of the death of an employee, one of our policyholders?"

"I'm not sure I buy into the coincidental aspect of the death, and I certainly don't think it's an accident that you happen to be researching AI threats. I think it's time you were more open with me."

"I think that might be a two-way street, Ms. Chen, so let me start by saying that I think you are looking for Kyrlos." He put that out there and just watched her. Her lips were slightly pursed, but she kept her poker face mostly intact.

"Should that mean something to me?" she asked indifferently.

"Well, I think it does, but if it doesn't, there is nothing to discuss, and I can finish my mundane insurance tasks." He made a move to swivel away to his laptop.

"How did you find out about Kyrlos?" she asked quietly.

"Elias Vance mentioned it in a memo he sent to Marcus Thorne, warning about security issues at Lunian Labs."

"That is interesting, but how did you see that memo?"

"I think I'll hold off on that detail for now, but I don't think it changes the information."

"Maybe I'll come back to that later."

"Why don't you tell me why you started looking for Kyrlos? And I'll tell you what I found out when I made contact with it." That did it. Chen actually reacted. The surprise was evident on her face. She got it under control quickly, but Alan smiled to let her know he saw it.

"Recently?" she asked.

"Last night. Briefly, but it was illuminating."

Ava Chen regarded him for several moments. The calculation behind her penetrating eyes was evident. She made a decision.

"I'll tell you, but this isn't a game, Alan. This is very serious."

"Ava, I know that. I am aware of the seriousness of the situation. I was terrified after talking to Kyrlos last night. Tell me how this started for you."

She seemed to gather herself for a few moments, thinking about where to start and how to tell her story. Taking a breath, she began to speak.

Ava Chen was at her desk in the National Cybersecurity and Communications Integration Center at St. Elizabeth's West Campus in Washington, DC. The center was new, having moved from its old location in Arlington a few years before. The NCCIC watch floor was a long, narrow space dominated by massive wall screens displaying various maps, real-time threat data, and network activity. Across from the screens were workstations for the host of analysts and other technical resources, who monitored cybersecurity and infrastructure threats and incidents. Ava's workstation was typical of the setup for senior analysts. Three monitors were arrayed in front of her, allowing her to view vast amounts of data. Today, she was reviewing security event data to look for any signs of unusual threat activity. She was working with the Financial Systems threat team, looking for anything unusual in banking and other financial system traffic. It was long, meticulous work, which more often than not resulted in no findings. But it was important work that had to be done.

Ava's desk phone rang, and she pressed the speaker phone button without looking at the caller ID.

"Ava Chen," she announced distractedly, still looking at the data on her screen.

"Ava, it's John Danforth. Do you have a moment?" John was another senior analyst; he and Ava frequently collaborated on each other's cases.

"Hi John, what can I help with?"

"I have been looking at some infrastructure traffic out of Ohio. I want to get a second set of eyes on it." Ava was suddenly alert and giving the call her full attention.

"Sure, just send it over to my station and I'll take a look. Anything you want to tell me about it?"

"No, not yet. I want to know if you see it, and what you make of it. Sending it now. Call me back." He rang off just as an email alert popped up on her monitor. She opened the email and clicked on the attached file.

From the look of the data, it appears to be from a power plant in central Ohio. She scrolled through the data. Nothing immediately jumped out at her, and she reached the end of the file and frowned at the screen. John Danforth wasn't an alarmist. If he saw something here, it was here. She started over and re-read the file. Midway through, she stopped, backed up, and re-read a section, then did so again. Something was off about the traffic she was seeing between two of the power plant systems. It looked like routine communication. Syncing data between two monitoring systems designed to monitor the thermal performance of the gas engine running on Natural Gas. The data transferred from one system to the backup should have been the same, and it was, until a critical point in the middle of the file, where the performance values were slightly off. Looking at the data more closely, she could see that there were slight differences in the data packets when the data was identical to the segment, compared to when it wasn't. As soon as the data was similar again, the data packets returned to their original format. She stopped reading and punched the redial button on her phone.

"You see it too," John said, without preamble.

"Someone intercepted the feed from the monitoring system in the middle of that communication segment and made subtle changes to the performance data. It was only for a few seconds. I almost didn't see it. It took me two readings to get it."

"Two! I read it four times until I figured out what was bugging me about it."

"Well, I had the advantage of knowing that you had already found something. Did you report this already?"

"Typing that out now that you confirmed it. I have re-reviewed the last two weeks of traffic at that plant, and this doesn't show up anywhere else."

"Feels like a probe, someone testing out their ability to affect the monitoring data."

"Yeah, that is what I got from it, too. Would you like to go with me to talk to Henry about it? I think someone should go out there and take a look. She agreed to go with him to see their boss, Henry Marcellous, and they decided to meet there in five minutes.

_____

Henry Marcellous, a burly man in his 60s, looked over their data and listened to their conclusions. He leaned back and considered it for a few minutes.

"I'm not sure I see a cyberattack here. It might be a simple malfunction in the syncing software. Have we even had a diagnostic run on that yet?"

"We can do that, Henry, and I will ask for the diagnostic immediately, but the data is too perfect, the results are off by tiny amounts, and they match up perfectly with the data packet differences. This was an outside system communicating with the second monitoring system, I would bet my life on it," John replied passionately.

Marcellous looked at Ava, "I'm not sure about my life, but I agree with John that the most likely explanation is that this was some kind of probing intrusion. Maybe a test of a new system. It doesn't look like a glitch to me, it's too perfect and almost undetectable."

"Well then. John, keep on the investigation here. Ava, get out to Ohio and do a site inspection on this power plant and see if you can find any more evidence of what we are dealing with."

John and Ava quickly thanked their boss for his time and left his office.

The following afternoon, Ava Chen stood in the Natural Gas Power Plant operations center in New Albany, Ohio. She was dressed in a charcoal suit, which had almost survived the flight from D.C. without wrinkling. She was quietly staring at the operations director as he gave her several reasons why there could be no intrusion in his systems. After a few moments, the intensity of her look made him uncomfortable enough to fade off in his objections.

"Director Curry, I'm sure your systems are state-of-the-art. This isn't an accusation about you or your people. This investigation examines the possibility of a malicious actor conducting tests to infiltrate the country's power grid. This is exactly the type of activity that CISA was created to protect against. Let's just run all the tests and see what comes back. My colleague, John Danforth, is back in Washington looking at data, and together we want to get a complete picture about what happened and try to figure out how to combat it." She stopped to give him time to process the situation. He did so, then nodded glumly in acceptance of her plan.

Hours later, with John's voice in her ear via a Bluetooth earbud, they found what they were looking for. For almost 15 seconds, an external connection had been established between the two monitoring systems, allowing data to flow through the data stream. It had been challenging to detect because the outside system had entered through another process unrelated to the monitoring systems and managed to compromise the network from that third system. Once inside the network, the intruder set up a virtual service that handled the actual attack. The attack wasn't perfect; a network monitor shut down the connection after 15 seconds.

"It's scary how close that came to being able to work," John said in her ear.

"It would have worked if the intruder were slightly better at masking its packet spoofing. It wouldn't take much to make this impossible to detect. We wouldn't have seen it at all."

"That's not a pleasant thought."

"We have the smoking gun; now we need to find out where it was fired from."

There was some typing on the other end of the connection as John Danforth searched through the massive amount of communication logs they had reviewed over the past few hours.

"There is a lot of routing going on in this stream. Curious, though several of the hops go through data centers connected to the same entity."

"Another target? Or the source?" she pondered as he worked.

"I don't know for sure, but I know you are going to Jacksonville."

"Florida? Who is the other party?"

"Lunian Labs. The trace doesn't go back to them directly. However, whoever was running this used a routine through their network for part of the way. I never got back to the destination."

"I guess I'm heading to the Sunshine State," Ava said, closing her laptop and tapping her earpiece to end the connection.

The following morning, she was in Elias Vance's office, the chief scientist of Lunian Labs. She had never met him but had heard his name before. He was widely regarded in CISA and was one of the voices of restraint in the AI community. Recognizing the threat of malicious individuals gaining access to highly advanced technology, he championed safety protocols and regulations.

"That's curious, Ms. Chen. For something to have been this effective, it would have to have very advanced digital twinning capabilities. I'm not aware of any systems in operation today that do so. It's theoretically possible, has been for a long time, but not achieved in any published work I know." Elias Vance was in his mid-fifties, but he looked a little older due to his perpetual state of weariness and his gaunt face.

"Any ideas where it might have come from?" Ava asked from the small desk chair in his office on the third floor of Lunian's offices in Jacksonville, FL.

"No, I really don't. I'll ask around and see what I can find. In this facility, the only group capable of working on such advanced technology would be the Advanced Research Division. You may want to speak with Director Georgia Jackson. I haven't heard about anything like this from their team, but she would know what prototypes they are working on."

"Thank you for your assistance, Mr. Vance. I'll talk to her. Let me know if you find anything," he said and shook her hand, assuring her he would be in contact.

Ava's conversation with Georgia Jackson was vague and inconclusive. Jackson assured her that her team wasn't working on anything related to digital twinning and indeed wasn't conducting any live tests in the field. While she seemed forthcoming and open, Ava couldn't shake the feeling that something about the interview was troubling Jackson.

Unable to shake the sense that someone at Lunian Labs knew more than they were saying, Ava walked out of the facility and headed back to her temporary offices downtown. Hoping Vance would reach out to her with more information.

"He never did, though," Ava concluded her story. "When I tried to contact him later in the week, the company told me he was on leave, and then you know the rest. Part of my follow-up investigation turned up the memo; his question about Kyrlos in it is the only clue. We haven't been able to find a trace of the system again." She finished, looking to Alan to fulfill his part of the bargain.

Alan reached into his desk drawer and pulled out a small pouch. He handed it over to Ava Chen, and she glanced inside but made no comment.

"That is the hard drive I was given by Georgia Jackson, and a flash drive containing data, and a program used to build a scenario to contact Kyrlos. I doubt the routine will work again; the system undoubtedly has put in more security after it detected the unauthorized connection." He paused to pass a piece of paper to the earnest analyst in front of his desk. The paper was an edited transcript of the conversation Layla had with Kyrlos. It had been altered to remove any mention of Layla.

"That is interesting, and terrifying," Ava said after reading the brief document. "Any ideas who Admin and DevOne are?"

"No, not really. I guess there are suspects. Jackson, Marksdale, and Salazar might still find a way to fit in somehow. Or possibly someone at Lunian we haven't considered yet."

"I will have my team analyze this data. See if we can find something you missed."

Layla made a noise in Alan's ear; he tried to keep his face blank, though he was smiling inside. "So, I will continue to ask questions and reach out to contacts. I will see if I can dig up anything on my end. We are going to continue to share?"

Ava hesitated, but only for a second, "Yes. I'll keep you in the loop with anything we find on the technical side, and you let me know what you find out with your investigation." She stood. Alan mirrored her action and put out a hand. She regarded him for a moment, then extended her hand and gave him a quick, firm shake. She nodded at him and turned to go.

Alan waited until she was out of sight down the hall, then reached into his center drawer and pulled Layla out and sat her on the top of the desk.

"What did you think, partner?"

"I think she is thawing to you," Layla said brightly.

"It's about time! Seriously, though, I think she is just highly committed to this case. Clearly, Kyrlos has the entire CISA spooked."

"After what has happened this week, it has me spooked as well."

"Where do we go from here?"

"I think we need to talk to Georgia Jackson again. Why did she omit the existence of the backup to Ava Chen? Who deleted the backup on their servers? There are so many unanswered questions."

"I'll call Lunian and see about making an appointment to speak to her."

Chapter Sixteen

EXPOSED

A lan sat at his desk in thought. He had not been successful in getting an appointment to see Georgia Jackson, director of the Advanced Research Division at Lunian Labs. He had managed to reach an assistant in the ARD, but she couldn't find a time in Jackson's schedule for today and suggested a date for the following week. Alan took the appointment, but was not happy about it.

Layla had been sitting on his desk, activity lights were steady but not agitated. She was working on re-reviewing all the data she had collected on the Kyrlos encounter. She was looking for any clues that might help her track down the AI system again and make another attempt to connect to it.

Alan ran his hand through his sandy hair in frustration, leaving it a bit disheveled. He made a decision. "Layla, I am going to go out to Lamina Labs and see if I can get a few minutes with Jackson. I want to know why she hid the backup from Ava."

"I think that is a good idea, Alan. I will continue to work on these log files. I am hoping there is something I am missing. You can leave me in the office. If I find anything, I'll communicate with you via the SmartLens glasses. They will also record any interview so that I won't miss anything."

"Okay, call if you need anything." There was no response, and when Alan looked down, Layla's light pattern indicated she was in deep concentration mode, the rapidly alternating lights he had seen before. He knew from that experience that she wouldn't respond until she was finished with her task. Grabbing the SmartLens glasses off the desk, he put them in his side jacket pocket and left the office, closing the door to give Layla privacy.

As he walked down the hall, he noticed Stacy was not at her desk. Before he could wonder where she was, he heard her on the stairs, coming up with an armload of mail and packages from the mailroom. Usually, they bring the deliveries up to her every day; they must have gotten behind, and she went to retrieve them. As he approached the stairs, she stumbled. Alan instinctively reached out to steady her. She jumped a little at his touch, and packages went flying everywhere.

"I'm so sorry, Stacy. I didn't mean to startle you."

She laughed as they both bent down to pick up packages, "My own fault, I was lost in my own little world and didn't know you were there."

As they deposited the packages on her desk, she asked him where he was off to.

"To Lunian Labs to see if I can force an appointment out of the director of the research division."

"Good Luck with that. And thanks for the help." He smiled at her and departed down the stairs.

Alan arrived at Lunian Labs late in the afternoon. The parking lot was still full of cars. He had a flash of regret that he hadn't had Layla look up what kind of car Georgia Jackson drove. Maybe it was a black sedan. Shrugging off the missed opportunity, he made a mental note to look into it later. He got out of the car and took the now-routine trek up to the visitor security station.

Inside, he asked the guard for Georgia Jackson, impressed upon him that it was critical that he see her today, and waited while the guard picked up the phone and spoke quietly for several minutes.

"I'm sorry, sir. Director Jackson is not in the office. She had an off-site appointment this afternoon and won't be back today. Her assistant informs me that you already have an appointment for next week."

"I don't suppose you can tell me where the offsite meeting is."

"I don't have that information, sir."

Alan thanked him and headed back to the car. As he approached the vehicle, he remembered Layla was back at the office and reached down to grab his SmartLens glasses. His heart stopped as he felt his empty jacket pocket. He patted other pockets irrationally, already knowing they weren't there. He tried to think of where he could have lost them. Quickly searching the car produced no results. He sat in the car thinking, and it came to him that they must have dropped out of his pocket when he bent down to help Stacy gather those dropped packages. He hurriedly put the car into gear and headed back to the office.

While he rushed back, Stacy sat at her desk typing some notes from a meeting she had attended earlier in the day. Her mind focused on the task. She was startled to see Jane Winston, one of the other assistants, at her desk, holding a pair of glasses. She gave her an inquiring look.

"I found these on the stairs. I don't know who they belong to," Jane said, holding them out to Stacy.

Taking them and looking at them carefully, Stacy replied, "Oh, these belong to Alan. He must have dropped them earlier. I'll get them back to him. Thanks, Jane." Jane waved and went back to her desk farther down the hall.

Stacy set the glasses on her desk and returned to her typing. The glasses were in her line of sight as she typed; her vision kept coming back to them every few seconds. Finally, curiosity too great to resist, she stopped her work and picked them up. They were clearly of excellent quality, light construction, and very stylish. She noticed the small cameras on the side of the lenses and marveled at how difficult they were to see. She opened the glasses and tried them. There was a quiet tone as the glasses powered on. Stacy was a little disappointed that they seemed like regular glasses; she wasn't sure what she expected.

"Alan, glad you are back." A smooth female voice suddenly emanated from the glasses. "I think I found something in the Kyrlos data. "

"Who are you?" Stacy asked a second later, after she regained her senses from the surprise. There was a startled sound from the other party, followed by silence for a long second, and then finally a reply.

"Uh, I am just a friend of Alan's. I was working on some data analysis for him. Do you know when he will be back?"

"Friend, huh? I never heard him mention you. "

"Does he mention all his friends?" There was a tone in the voice now.

"Well, he clearly doesn't," Stacy replied. A noise pulled her attention to the stairs, and she saw Alan stop in his tracks, his mouth open in surprise as he looked at her wearing the glasses.

"Stacy…" he started.

"I think you've been hiding something from me, Alan."

He sighed, holding his hand out for the glasses. He said with resignation, "Let's talk in my office."

As they walked into his office, Stacy's eyes were immediately glued to Layla's smooth form sitting on his desk. The activity lights around her middle were flashing in an agitated manner.

"That is the object from the mysterious package. What is it?" Stacy asked. Alan had been thinking about his response during the long walk down the hallway. He had weighed the risks of trying to stonewall her or trying to lie his way out of the discovery. The risks were too significant, though, that she would talk unless she had a reason not to, and deep down, he trusted her.

"This is Layla. Layla, this is Stacy. I believe you spoke to her a few minutes ago."

"Good Afternoon, Stacy. I'm pleased to be introduced to you." The same smooth voice was coming from the small device on the desk. Stacy's eyes widened. She looked to Alan for an explanation.

"Layla is an incredibly advanced artificial intelligence agent. Since she came to me last week, we have been working together to solve a mystery. It involves her existence, her being sent to me, and lately some untimely deaths."

"That is incredible!"

"She is a very special person," Alan said, looking at Layla.

"You said deaths." Stacy wrinkled her brow, "More than the car accident?"

"Yes, there was another man, Elias Vance. He is the scientist who created Layla and sent her to me. He died before Hector Villenuez."

"I read about him in the Times," Stacy replied slowly. "It said he committed suicide."

"Yes, the scene looked like that, but there were other factors that made that very unlikely. Layla and I believe he was murdered. We have been looking into his death and some other things going on. Vance left us a message that makes us believe someone was trying to take Layla from him before he died. He asked me to protect her. And now, I am asking you the same thing. Help me protect her. She has capabilities that could be used to do great harm, and the people after her do not care about her best interests."

"What do you need me to do?"

"First, you can't mention her to anyone. Ever," she nodded gravely. "After that, just do what you always do and do your best to help me." Her face broke into a warm grin.

"I can do that. I always do."

Alan nodded in agreement, then paused to consider what would happen next. Layla chimed in to help him out.

"Perhaps I could bring Stacy up to speed on the investigation. If she is going to help, and keep our confidence, she should know what has happened, who the players are, and what the dangers are." Stacy looked expectantly at Alan for a decision.

"That is an excellent idea, Layla. Stacy, do you have a Bluetooth headset?" In answer, she reached into the pocket of her designer jeans and produced a carrying case for a pair of Bose earbuds.

"Great. Put them on, and Layla will pair with them so she can communicate with you."

Excitedly, Stacy donned the earbuds and waited patiently for Layla to pair with them. Once that was completed, Alan could hear the faint sound of Layla's voice coming from the buds. Stacy acknowledged she could listen to her.

"Go ahead and return to your desk; Layla will brief you. Ask her whatever questions come up. And welcome to the team."

Stacy hugged him quickly and a little awkwardly and almost dashed out of the office, peppering Layla with questions as she went. Alan sighed, hoping his instincts were right. Stacy could be a great asset to the team, but there were risks. The more people who knew about Layla's existence, the harder it would be to protect her.

Chapter Seventeen
CORPORATE ESPIONAGE

The following morning, Layla was waiting patiently for Alan to awake. As he stumbled out out of the bedroom and into the kitchen to make coffee, she greeted him and jumped right in to give him an update.

"Yesterday was so chaotic, I didn't get a chance to tell you my findings about Kyrlos."

Yawning, Alan replied. "Sorry about that, partner. What did you find out?"

"I analyzed all the network traffic related to the encounter with Kyrlos. There are distinct markers in the packets it generates in their responses. With the right search algorithm and access to enough data, I think it could eventually be tracked down."

"That is great news! What do we need to do?" he asked, sipping his coffee.

"I can write the algorithm. That is already in progress, but I don't have nearly the access I need to find Kyrlos. We are going to need someone with a lot more access to run this query."

"You're talking about CISA."

"I am afraid so. I can prepare the script they will need, but they will have to run it. I assume that before they agree to run it, they will have to vet the whole thing with their own coders. That will take time, but assuming they will share the results with us, it might help us track it down. I need a little time once they have to try to isolate it."

"Finish the code, and I'll handle Ava and CISA. How was your catch-up session with your new bestie?"

Layla actually groaned in response. "She really is a sweet young woman, but she is way too enthusiastic!"

"She means well, and she might be useful. Stacy has a talent for research. We might put that to good use."

"She already offered to look through all of Adamant's records on Lunian policies to see if we have missed anything, or if there is information that we haven't seen yet."

"Oh, speaking of chaos interrupting. I meant to ask you if you could check on what kind of car Georgia Jackson drives."

"I'll check the available DMV records and get back to you. Now, let's get a shower and get moving. I want to see what Stacy has uncovered. While you get ready, I will finish this script for CISA."

Alan stopped at Stacy's desk and put a large latte and a blueberry muffin down in front of her. She looked up from her screen; her eyes grew big, and she pounced on the muffin. In between bites, she thanked him with her mouth full of food. Reddening with embarrassment.

"Sorry," she mumbled. Alan waved away her apology.

"Any progress on the research?"

"Nothing definite yet. I'm making my way through a mountain of data we have on Lunian. They have several policies with us. It's a lot of files to review. I'll let you know what I find."

Alan nodded and smiled at her, then took his own coffee and muffin to his office. Sitting at his desk, he began crafting the email to Ava Chen. Layla had emailed him the script on the drive into work. He just had to include a cover letter and submit it to Ava and the rest of CISA, hoping they would be motivated to help. As he sent the message, he asked Layla what she was working on.

"Transcribing notes for a meeting for Stacy." Alan raised his eyebrow at this disclosure, and Layla responded, "It's the least I can do; she is doing research for us." He nodded his understanding.

Alan's cell phone vibrated in his pocket. Fishing it out, he recognized the number as one from the FDLE Crime Lab. Curious, he answered and identified himself.

"Alan, it's Mike Hughes. I wanted to share some information with you. It might be relevant for your claim."

"That sounds promising. What is it?"

"Hector Villenuez wasn't conscious when the car crashed. Autopsy results say he was asleep or unconscious when it hit. There were no defensive posture injuries. He never reacted to brace for impact. The ruling is that he was unconscious from unknown causes at the time of death."

Alan gave a low whistle. "That's pretty big news, Mike. Thanks for calling to let me know."

"Figured it might be important in your case. Have a good day." He disconnected, and Alan pondered the significance of this development. The steering wheel was pulled dramatically to the right just before the crash. If Villenuez didn't jerk the wheel, who did? Was someone else in the car? How could they have survived the crash? Something wasn't adding up, but then it all fell into place.

"Layla, we have another problem."

"What is it, Alan?"

"That was Mike Hughes with the FDLE. They just determined that Hector Villeunez was unconscious when the car crashed." Layla's activity lights flashed for several seconds.

"That means..." Layla started to say, but couldn't even finish the thought.

"Kyrlos killed Hector Villenuez." Hearing it outside his head made it even more shocking.

"Alan, if Kyrlos is capable of taking over an automobile and intentionally killing a human being, it is incredibly dangerous. It would not just be theoretically dangerous, should it get access to my abilities, but potentially deadly to any human with whom it comes into contact. It has no internal restraints on human life. AI doesn't have natural empathy. Without specific training to instill safeguards, Kyrlos will kill anyone who is in its way."

"They were hacked!" Stacy shouted from the doorway.

"Who was?" Layla and Alan asked in unison.

"Lunian Labs. They have a cybersecurity policy with us. They are required to report any incidents that resulted in any breach. Three months ago, there was a breach in one of their servers. The report states that the issue was brief and resolved, and additional measures were implemented. But I thought it was important." She stopped, waiting for their reaction.

"It is very important, Stacy. Excellent work," Layla reassured her new friend.

"Yes, great job, Stacy," Alan said. Stacy beamed at the praise.

"We'll take it from here. Send those reports to Alan's email, and I'll look at them and see where else that leads us." Stacy practically bounced out of the office. Alan couldn't help but grin at her enthusiasm.

"I need to talk to Marcus Thorne again. He never mentioned any cyberattack; clearly, Ava didn't know about it either, which means they never reported it to CISA. They are covering something up at the lab." He grabbed his desk phone to call Lunian Labs. At this point, he thought he should program them into his speed dial.

Marcus Thorne looked haggard and a little defiant as Alan entered his expansive executive office at Lunian Labs.

"This is a lot of follow-up for a car crash investigation, Mr. Harrison," Marcus said with a bit of heat in his voice.

"I think we both know that it is a lot more than a car crash, Thorne." Alan had dropped the overly polite customer service voice he had been using with the executive in previous meetings and was putting an edge in his voice.

"What are you talking about?"

"Tell me about the cyberattack." This shook Thorne a bit.

"What about it. It was nothing. Some ransomware attempt, I'm sure. We mitigated the intrusion and adjusted our firewalls to address the specific vulnerability it was attempting to exploit. Never happened again." He looked down at his hands as he spoke.

"It was more than that. They took something, or they attempted to take something."

"No, no, you are wrong. They didn't get anything."

"Then what was it? Clearly, it was something. You have two dead bodies, a missing contractor, and employees covering up concerned memos." Marcus sighed.

"They didn't take anything. They inserted something." Alan's mouth hung open for a second.

"What kind of something? How big?"

"It was tiny. We assumed it was some spider designed to steal information from our servers. We found it and killed it."

"I feel there is a but..."

"We were never able to determine what it was actually supposed to be doing. It was very complex, and we couldn't break the encryption to get at the code. Then it vanished."

"Vanished? While you were working on it?"

"We had a top engineer on it, and one night the code just wasn't there anymore."

"I would ask you who it was, but I already know, don't I?"

"Yes, Hector Villenuez was trying to access the code when the file vanished."

"How soon after the cyber incident did Howard Salazar show up?"

Startled, Thorne stared at him for several seconds, "I don't know exactly. Not long after that, probably a week or so."

"It didn't occur to you that Salazar was here looking for the code that was inserted?"

"Well, it does now. But that code didn't execute. We caught it in time, unless..."

"Unless Villenuez or Salazar activated it while they were trying to break into it."

"Yes. I hadn't considered that before today." He was deflated.

"You have to report this to CISA," Alan said. Thorne grimaced but nodded.

"You also have to find out what happened in your network when they activated it."

"We have been looking at every log we can get our hands on, or reconstruct, for weeks. There is nothing."

"Keep looking, and call CISA. I am going to report this conversation to one of their analysts. You should get ahead of that."

Marcus Thorne didn't get up when Alan left his office. He sat at his desk staring down at his hands.

Alan stopped by the front desk to inquire about Georgia Jackson again, but she was still not in and was not expected back until the following Monday. His existing appointment was for Monday afternoon. He left unsatisfied and more uneasy than when he arrived. What exactly was happening at Lunian? It was a lot more complicated than it initially seemed. It was more than just some rogue programmer writing code that got out of hand. This was much bigger.

Chapter Eighteen

Ambushed

Alan and Layla discussed his meeting with Marcus Thorne over pizza at Rojas Pizza. They sat in the crowded restaurant, with a view of the elephantine county courthouse across the street. Alan folded the giant slice of pepperoni and ate slowly, watching the foot traffic to and from the massive court building.

"So the real question is, who inserted the code into Lunian's server? Was it Howard Salazar? Or someone he is working with?"

"Or, is Kyrlos operating independently?" Alan asked between bites.

Layla considered this for a moment. "That would make sense. We know that Kyrlos can navigate the internet independently. Inserting itself into servers and operating there undetected. It has done that at least twice now. What about this scenario? Kyrlos feels threatened wherever it was originally hosted and moved into Lunian's server. Howard followed it there.

Hector Villenuez is just a bystander, or an unwitting tool for Kyrlos."

"That could work. But what happened to Howard? Did he kill Vance?"

"I don't know. It seems that Kyrlos killed Villenuez to prevent him from talking any more than he already had. I'm not sure what motive Salazar had for killing Vance or what happened to him afterwards."

"We need to find Georgia and find out what she knows about this. She is missing for a reason. I can feel it." Alan finished his slice and wiped the grease from his lips.

"Stacy and I are working on it," Layla assured him. "She is pulling every record she can find on Georgia Jackson, and I am looking at all the public records. She has an apartment on the west side, but the security company logs I was able to find don't show any entry there for the past few days. Wherever she is, it isn't at her apartment."

"Security logs seem pretty non-public," he replied.

"Um...well, there was an issue with the log server at the security company. I didn't do anything to create the breach, but I might have peeked at the available data while the vulnerability was unresolved."

"Your rationalizations are getting more creative," he observed.

"I told you I was capable of learning new abilities," she replied.

"Well, I have to go have an uncomfortable conversation with Ava. She needs to know about Villenuez's death, and she needs to know about the cyberattack, assuming Thorne hasn't told her yet. At this point, it's even money on that." Alan got up from the table.

"Don't forget to feed the troops!" Layla called out as he headed to the door; he snapped his fingers and headed back to the counter to get a slice of pizza for their hardworking assistant back at the office.

As he approached the Charles E. Bennett Federal Building, Alan took note of the colossal structure of beige and brown concrete. It was blocky and imposing, a testament to its 1960s-era design. Even a renovation just a couple of decades ago couldn't erase the monument's bureaucratic symbolism.

Alan felt a little exposed. He had not wanted to risk bringing Layla into the Federal Building, so he left her back on his desk. She continued to work with Stacy to dig up potential locations for Georgia Jackson. He had tried in vain to get Ava Chen to meet him on neutral ground, but she had insisted on the meeting taking place in her office.

Checking in at the desk downstairs, he registered as a visitor and waited for an escort. A very young man in an ill-fitting gray suit arrived and escorted him to the fourth-floor office, where

Ava Chen was sitting at a small desk, reading something on a laptop. She was dressed as usual in a dark power suit, her hair immaculately secured behind her head. Her eyes scanned the laptop screen, raised briefly, and took note of her visitor, then went back to their task. She ignored him for a couple of minutes until she finished whatever she was working on. Completing her work, she closed the laptop and sat back in her chair to assess Alan, who was seated in a small chair to the left of the desk.

"Who was the high school freshman who escorted me up here?" he asked. She shrugged.

"I have no idea, intern probably. What do you have for me?" While she was noticeably thawing to Alan, she was still all business. The consistency was a little maddening, but Alan had to admit he admired her for it.

Alan briefed her on the autopsy findings that she could almost certainly obtain for herself. Then he gave her a detailed report of his meeting with Marcus Thorne, the CEO of Lunian Labs. She listened to both stories passively without interruption. When he was done, she compiled it all in her mind before speaking.

"You're an analyst?" she asked. He nodded in confirmation. "For an analyst, you aren't all that bad at investigation." Alan felt this was high praise given her penchant for terse, no-frills communication.

"These are unusual times." That was all he said in reply. She seemed to appreciate him not making a big deal about the compliment.

"I saw the report on Villenuez, but I admit I hadn't had time to speculate about the AI being the killer, but it tracks. The cyber incident at Lunian is troubling. They should have reported that. What is your theory there?"

"I think Kyrlos originated outside of Lunian. I think it was inserted there either by Howard Salazar or someone else, or it put itself there on its own. It seems to be moving around to avoid detection."

"Do you think Salazar is capable of writing the code for Kyrlos?"

"You're more of an expert there than I am."

"He's smart, but he isn't known for breakthroughs like this. I guess it only takes one, though, to make a name for yourself," she admitted ruefully.

"I'm not sure. I think he was trying to contain it. I think he is chasing it; whether he had anything to do with development, I can't say. What about Cognixion? Have you looked into them?"

"Yes, but they aren't much more than Salazar. A couple of support personnel, including some lawyers and clerical staff. We didn't turn up any development teams. It could all be outsourced."

"Salazar worked at other companies, as a consultant and an employee, right?"

"Yes, he was at Apex a long time ago and formed his own company after that. Worked for OpenAI, Google, Aethera Dynamics, Anthropic, all the names in the industry at one time or another."

"Any one of those could have been the source of Kyrlos," Alan pointed out.

Ava nodded absently. "We are still looking for traces of the system based on the research you gave us. How did you come by all that?"

Layla had prepared him for this question. They knew it would come sooner or later. "I studied the industry a bit in college, and I've kept up with it. I'm not an expert at it or anything, but I still know my way around Wireshark." He paused, hoping that name-dropping the open-source internet packet tool would sound authentic. Ava nodded, accepting his explanation and moving on.

"Well, you've made more progress than we have. I am going to visit Lunian and obtain their data on this breach. And I am going to see if I can get more people in D.C. to participate in the packet search for Kyrlos. Let me know if you find anything else." Her tone was pleasant, but it was clear that he was being dismissed. Alan gave her a lovely smile and got up. He didn't offer a hand, and she didn't seem to expect it. He waved from the door, and she nodded back at him as he left. The intern was waiting just outside the door to escort him back down to the lobby and out the door.

Getting back behind the wheel of his Orion Chimera, he picked up his SmartLens glasses from where he had left them in the console. Putting them on, he hit the Start button and pulled away from the curb. There was a polite cough in his ear. Smiling at her newfound caution, Alan answered.

"Yes, it's really me, Layla."

"Glad to hear your voice. We have something for you. Come by and pick us up."

"Us?"

"Yes, I have news, and Stacy did most of the work, so she wants to tell you. And we both want to get out of the office."

"Screaming Goat Coffee it is."

In the late afternoon, the clientèle had thinned out considerably at the coffee shop. Stacy and Alan sat at a corner table, each with their respective drinks: her latte and his steaming Americano.

"I don't know how he drinks that stuff. It's like drinking molten lava," Stacy observed.

"I think he thinks it makes him look tough," Layla said, connected to both the SmartLens glasses and Stacy's Bluetooth earbuds.

"I'm sitting right here. I like my coffee pure and not polluted by organic soy juice," he said, looking at Stacy's drink. She sipped it and shot back.

"It's almond milk." Alan's shrug showed he didn't see the difference.

"So, what do you have?" Alan asked.

"Stacy found it," Layla said with a touch of pride. Alan looked to Stacy.

"It was really just luck. After I found the cyberattack report, I found a memo from the adjuster. He noted that he wanted to require Lunian to update its documentation listing all the locations where data could be accessed. So, I pulled those forms that were updated a month ago, and five pages in, I found a listing for a vacation club home. Apparently, it is used by executives. I almost ignored it, but there was nothing else to check, so I mentioned it to Layla."

"I checked records on it, and it hasn't been used recently. No one is supposed to be there. This made it really suspicious that there was electrical usage showing up for that property. Not background levels, the type of usage you would see if someone were living there."

"Where is it?" Alan asked.

"Beachfront on Jekyll Island in Georgia," Stacy supplied cheerily.

"You think Georgia Jackson might be there?" he asked them both.

"I think it is worth a trip out there to find out. It's about an hour north of the city."

"This is good work, by both of you."

"When do we leave?" Stacy asked, her voice filled with excitement.

"You aren't going," Alan said firmly.

"Aww."

"No, I'm going alone."

"You are not," Layla said firmly.

"Alright," Alan conceded, "I'm taking Layla, but she is staying in the car."

"Can I drive?"

"We'll see. I'll take you both to dinner first, then we'll drop Stacy off at her car, and we'll head out. Stacy, we'll give you a play-by-play in the morning. Good work today, really. Thank you." She was still disappointed, but the praise lifted her spirits as did the prospect of dinner company.

By the time they had finished dinner at a seafood restaurant on the St. John's River, and he had dropped Stacy off at her car, the sun was setting. He drove the 75 miles up Interstate 95 to the exit for Jekyll Island, arriving after dark.

The Island was 9 square miles and filled with quaint mid-century modern architecture. It was once the vacation retreat for a who's who of the American wealth class. The State of Georgia now manages it, and it has become a popular tourist destination. Much of the beachfront property was now owned by hotel chains, but there were still residential districts in some parts of the island. The vacation home maintained by Lunian Labs was in one of those areas. The address Layla supplied was at the end of a long street, nestled among a copse of Cabbage Palm trees. A small, two-story, painted brick house with a minimalist traditional design stood there. As he parked the car near the road and got out, Alan could hear and smell the beach just over the dunes to the east. A late-model red Toyota was parked in the driveway.

"I'm a little disappointed it isn't a black sedan," he said as he passed by it.

"That would be too easy," Layla said via the SmartLens speakers.

"Something in this case should be," she replied with a sympathetic sound.

Alan walked up to the door and knocked. He almost expected no answer, but after a beat or two, the door opened and there she was. Georgia Jackson, dressed in jeans and a sweatshirt. She looked at him with a sour expression.

"There goes my quiet weekend," she said and stepped aside to let him enter.

"I'll try not to make it any more painful than it has to be," he said, walking past her and entering the house.

Just past a modest-sized foyer was a tastefully, if minimally decorated, living room. The large screen TV was on, but the picture was frozen, paused when Alan had knocked on the door. Without offering him anything, Georgia sat down on the couch. Alan chose a comfortable chair across from her.

"You're a hard woman to find."

"Not hard enough, obviously," She replied lightly.

"Why are you in hiding?"

"I'm not. I was feeling stressed and decided to take a few days to unwind."

"I don't really blame you for being stressed, dead bodies are stacking up, and your boyfriend seems to be knee deep in it." She regarded him coldly.

"I don't know what I would call Tom at the moment, but boyfriend doesn't seem to fit."

Alan shrugged, indicating he wasn't hung up on the description, "I was a little surprised when the CISA analyst working this case for the government didn't know that you had given me a backup of Hector Villenuez's machine."

"She didn't ask, and her bedside manner didn't leave me feeling chatty."

"I get that, Ava takes some getting used to. That's it? Nothing else going on there?"

"No. I guess I assumed she would ask about it sooner or later. I didn't think that much about it."

"Georgia, do you know what Kyrlos really is?" she shook her head.

"I really don't. I suspect Tom knows more than he is saying, but I don't know how much more."

"Is there any chance he wrote a sophisticated AI system capable of autonomous activity?"

"I doubt it. He is a good engineer, maybe even a great one, but he isn't a visionary."

"Tell me about the breach." She looked surprised for a moment.

"I suspect you know as much as I do by now. Someone breached our network a couple of months ago and installed spyware on one of our servers. It was detected by our intrusion systems quickly and isolated. Hector was assigned to try to reverse-engineer the code to determine what it was doing and who had placed it there. It vanished off the server before he could."

"It vanished. And Kyrlos showed up," Alan said it flatly.

"Yes. Kyrlos showed up later. I assumed Howard was responsible for that."

"You don't think the two are connected?" Her face suggested she hadn't thought about it like that.

"You mean, the spyware was related to the creation of Kyrlos?" she asked, puzzled.

"Yes. What if Hector didn't fail? What if he and Howard Salazar succeeded in cracking the encryption, but doing so released Kyrlos?" Her eyes widened. Alan could see her going over it in her head.

"Tom," she said softy, to herself.

"What about him?"

"Tom gave Hector space in a remote data center. It was supposed to be isolated from our main networks. It was being prepped for a pre-training job we were going to start early next year. He mentioned to me a week or so ago that Hector was bugging him for more and more processing power to try to get into the package."

"Where is the data center?" Layla asked in his ear. He relayed the question to Georgia.

"Between Jacksonville and Gainesville. The middle of nowhere, like most of those sites."

"So that's it?" he asked. "There isn't anything else? You really aren't hiding out?"

She laughed, "No, I'm just a tired woman watching Netflix and catching her breath." She waved at the paused TV.

"You still plan to be back in the office on Monday?"

"Yes. Do you still need the appointment you've been harassing everyone to set up for you?"

"I don't know. Let's see how the weekend goes." She shook her head, but chuckled a little. Alan couldn't think of anything else to ask her, and he wanted to get Layla's take on the data center. He thanked Georgia for her time and got up to leave. She walked him to the door and let him out.

Alan paused on the other side of the door for a moment, then walked out toward the street and his car. The light from the porch went off behind him, and the yard was plunged into darkness. Alan felt, rather than heard, movement behind him, and as he started to turn, something blunt and heavy struck him behind the left ear. He felt his legs crumble beneath him, and he went down hard.

Layla heard him fall. From the car's console, her own sensors couldn't see anything, but she had access to the Chimera systems. The 360 cameras showed a shadowy figure in the darkness leaning over Alan, going through his pockets. Alan was moving, but lethargically as if he was in slow motion or encased in quicksand. She felt a moment of desperation, then decided on a course of action.

The Chimera systems came to life, and the car jumped the curb and drove rapidly across the grass toward Alan and the shadowy figure. The horn let out a screech, and the headlights flashed in a blinding pattern. The figure over Alan looked up in a panic. The figure's face was obscured, and Layla could tell nothing about whoever was beneath the dark clothing, mask, and gloves. The Chimera kept coming. The figure played chicken with her as late as it dared, but ultimately was spooked by the noise and the onrushing 5000 pounds of metal.

The figure took off just as the Chimera arrived at Alan and almost managed to get away, but was clipped by the front fender. It stumbled, recovered, and ran down the street, out of sight. Layla swerved the car to the side and presented the passenger-side door to Alan, activating the lock; it popped open. Alan was still struggling to get to his feet. He was, though, still wearing his SmartLens glasses. Layla pumped up the volume, bypassing the safety settings, and shouted in his ear. "ALAN! GET UP!" His head snapped back at the sound, and he managed to drag himself into the passenger seat. Layla accelerated, and the momentum slammed the door shut.

As she made the turn onto the street, she saw the confused and alarmed face of Georgia Jackson at the open front door of the vacation home. Layla didn't waste time thinking about her; she floored the accelerator and navigated the car out of the residential neighborhood and onto the main road off the island. She tried talking to Alan, but his adrenaline had carried him as far as it could, and he had succumbed to the darkness. He lay unconscious in the seat as the car sped down the highway.

Layla dialed a number. "Hello?" Stacy Collins' sleepy voice came on the phone.

"Stacy, it's Layla. I need your help."

CHAPTER NINETEEN

HACKING

S tacy Collins, wearing a hastily put-together outfit of sweatpants and a baggy T-shirt, waited nervously in front of her apartment building. The Brooklyn was a vivid orange, lemon-yellow, and chartreuse-green contemporary apartment building that had been built in an old Riverside district a few years ago. The dark Chimera coupe appeared out of the darkness and screeched to a stop in front of her. Stacy could see Alan slumped in the front seat. He didn't seem to be moving.

"Get in the back seat!" Layla demanded in her ear. She complied, jumping into the back behind Alan. As the car leaped away from the curb, she leaned over the seat to examine her friend.

"Alan? Can you hear me?" he mumbled a response that she didn't really understand. "Layla, what happened?"

"He was attacked outside the vacation home on the island."

"Attacked? By whom?"

"I don't know. It was dark, and the figure was dressed in black."

A few seconds later, the coupe pulled up to the entrance to the Emergency Room at the nearby hospital. Stacy jumped out of the car, opened the front passenger door and gently shook Alan awake. His eyes tried to focus on her, but didn't quite succeed. Despite this, she was able to get him to climb out of the car, and she supported him as they walked to the brightly lit glass doors of the hospital. The doors opened up automatically as they approached, and she guided him inside to a chair. She checked him in, describing the attack as a mugging, and waited for him to be seen.

After what seemed like a century, but was really only a couple of hours, they came and took him back. She went with him, taking the SmartLens glasses from him and putting them on herself. She watched as they examined him, took his vitals, and administered cognitive tests. By the time they were seen, Alan was more conscious, and although he was exhausted, he was able to answer questions and pass the concentration and cognition exam.

The doctor informed them that Alan had a mild concussion, gave Stacy instructions for the next 24 hours, and told her to watch him for signs of a more serious condition. After more than four hours, they were released.

The automatic doors of the Emergency Room opened, and Stacy supported Alan as he slowly walked out onto a covered walkway between the ER and the Ambulance bay. Alan mumbled his thanks again for what seemed like the hundredth time. Stacy shushed him and told him to concentrate on walking.

Their destination was the dark Orion Chimera coupe parked silently at the curb across from the hospital. Remembering that she was wearing Alan's SmartLens glasses, Stacy called out to Layla.

"Incoming."

"I'm ready. Get him into the backseat. The connection inside the hospital was very unreliable. What did the doctors say?"

"No permanent injury. Mild concussion. He needs rest."

"That's a relief."

Stacy got him loaded into the backseat and started to open the driver's side door. But received a rebuke. "Not on your life. Stay with him, I'll take care of the driving."

Stacy climbed into the back seat next to Alan and buckled her seatbelt. He was already dozing off next to her. Layla fired up the Chimera and got it moving. The drive to Alan's house was short; it was only a half dozen blocks away from the hospital. Layla mused that it might be convenient if he was going to make a habit of getting knocked unconscious.

Layla expertly navigated the car into the driveway in front of the house. Stacy got out, retrieved Layla from the front console, then gently woke Alan and helped him out of the car. As they approached the front door, Layla activated the keypad, and the lock disengaged. Stacy maneuvered them into the house. She had never been to Alan's place before, and she stood inside the door, taking in the room and wondering where she was going.

"Upstairs, on the left," Layla provided, sensing her question.

Stacy helped Alan up the stairs. He was moving a little better, but he was still groggy. In the bedroom, she got him sitting on the bed and looked around. His sleeping clothes were folded neatly on a chair. Looking at him slumped slightly on the bed, she sighed and reached for them.

"Well, we are going to get a lot more acquainted, I guess," Stacy said. He grunted, but didn't say anything. Slowly, she helped him out of his clothes. She paused when she found the holstered pistol on his belt. She unclipped it and put it in the nightstand drawer. Helping him out of his shoes, shirt, and jeans, she got him into the oversized t-shirt and silky running shorts. That was a lot of work for him, and he was obviously exhausted by the effort. She pulled back the comforter and sheet, then helped him into bed. He settled back on the pillow and closed his eyes. She watched him for a moment.

"Stop watching me sleep, go home," he mumbled to her. He opened one eye slightly, then, realizing that it took more energy than he had, closed it again. Stacy rested a hand on his shoulder for a moment. He covered her hand with his and was asleep in under a minute.

Wandering downstairs, Stacy found Layla sitting on the dining room table where she had been set down as they came into the house. Her LEDs were flashing rapidly and agitatedly.

"He's asleep," Stacy announced.

"Good. I was terrified. I appreciate your help."

"You're welcome. What are you going to do now?"

"I don't know. I let him down; he could have been killed. I should have figured out we were in danger."

"How could you know that, you don't even know who attacked him?"

"I should, though, I should be doing more. I have been holding back, trying not to overuse my abilities. Worried about the ethics of intrusion into private data. I can't shake the notion that if I had been more ruthless in this investigation, he wouldn't have gotten hurt."

"You don't know that. And even if it were true, obsessing about it now won't do anyone any good."

"You're right. I am going to put all that behind me and get to work. I have a lot of tracing to do. Do you want me to drive you home?" Stacy looked surprised.

"I'm not leaving! The doctor said to watch him to make sure his concussion symptoms don't get worse."

"I have state-of-the-art environmental sensors and 360-degree cameras. I can watch him."

"You are going to be occupied with your hackathon. I'll stay and keep an eye on him. Call me if you need anything." She started for the stairs.

"Before you go, put me on the charging station next to the couch. I am going to be using a lot of processing power." Stacy complied, picking up Layla's compact form and carrying her into the living room, where she put her down on the thin Qi charging pad on the side table. As she did, she noticed a bookcase along the room's wall and went over to it.

She was impressed by the wide variety of titles on the shelves, ranging from non-fiction tomes on insurance and technical subjects to acclaimed prize-winning novels and numerous mystery novels. She picked up a slim paperback copy of Elmore Leonard's *The Switch*, examined the back cover for a moment, then carried it with her upstairs.

Layla watched Stacy ascend the staircase carrying her book. Then, pausing to organize her thoughts, she dug into her task. From the start of this case, several people obviously fit into the puzzle somehow, but they hadn't quite figured out where all of them went. The best place to start, she decided, was with a timeline. Knowing that Alan would eventually want to see her work, she powered up the 80-inch TV in the living room and connected her video output to it. She started placing key dates and times onto the timeline. As each point was placed, it appeared on the screen. It began with the intrusion into Lunian's data center, Howard Salazar's arrival in town, the incident at the Ohio power station, Elias Vance's memo, Vance's death, the chase and attack on her in the car, and Hector's death. She kept going until she got to the attack on Alan outside the vacation house on Jekyll Island.

Having completed the first part of the timeline, she went back and reviewed each person of interest who had come within the scope of the investigation.

Layla had to make some decisions about where to draw the line between her ethical positions on privacy and the greater good of the case. Up until now, except for emergencies that required gaining access to investigation spaces, such as Vance's apartment and Lunian, she had avoided private data sources. She started with Vance. Figuring that getting killed gave her higher moral justification to violate his privacy, she expanded her search to his private data. Vance's Car GPS placed him on the southside at an apartment building called Satori Town Center the day he died. She searched the database of the apartment complex, but couldn't find anything conclusive. Too much activity in their security system to nail down exactly which apartment he had been in, and the security cameras weren't working for some reason.

Next, she added Rhonda Winters to the timeline. She couldn't really find any reason to label her a suspect. She relied on public data and outlined all the known locations for Winters over the past two months. Winters had an active professional calendar. She had attended conferences, spoken on panels, and been interviewed on TV; many of those incidents overlapped with the timeline. On the night of Vance's death, she was speaking at a symposium in San Diego about how AI needed to advance to take the next step in advanced robotics. Tonight, she was in Los Angeles, attending an industry awards ceremony.

Rhonda had given them the name of Howard Salazar as a potential interview candidate; she added him to the timeline. He was definitely seriously involved in this case. There was far too much smoke for there to be no flame. She labeled him a suspect and started tracking his movements. He had been in Northern California just before the data center breach. The offices of Cognixion were there. He flew to Jacksonville three days after the break-in. That fit roughly with the timeline Marcus Thorne had given them. Salazar rented a dark blue BMW 7 series; as far as she could tell from the data, he still had it. He had several bank accounts for personal and business use; she found credit card purchases around the area. She mapped out all of the locations.

Hector Villenuez's name had come up the night of their search of Lunian Labs. His role with the ARD and the suspicion that they were somehow involved with Kyrlos made him a suspect. She started searching his social and banking data. No social activity she could see, but she found some very interesting details in his financial data. Before the intrusion into Lunian Labs' data center, he had been very predictable, making regular purchases at the exact locations each day along his route to and from work. That changed after the intrusion. Shortly after the incident, he started traveling in a wider circle. She ended up with a map showing all of the locations he had made small food or beverage purchases in the past month. They were spread out all over the area. Gainesville, Lake City, St. Augustine, Palm

Coast. She made a note to correlate all of those with any relevant businesses or facilities.

Examining the map, she noticed that after the intrusion, Howard Salazar's movements frequently lined up with Hector Villenuez. They were traveling together often, until after Vance's death.

Next, she added Georgia Jackson and Thomas Marksdale. They were not, as far as she could tell, real suspects right now, but something was troubling about Marksdale. Deciding to split the difference, she looked at Marksdale's financial data. The one worrisome thing she found was a gasoline purchase along the route from Jacksonville to Jekyll Island. The purchase had occurred earlier in the day, but could he have still been there and attacked Alan outside the house?

Marcus Thorne wasn't an actual suspect, but he did have some answers he needed to provide. Layla walked a fine line with him, looking at records from Lunian's internal data, but not private banking data. His calendar had meetings with several of the subjects, including Jackson and Marksdale, after the break. He met with Salazar multiple times over the next week, and Vance the day before his death. His phone logs showed a phone call to Rhonda Winters the day after the news broke about Vance's death.

As the night and early morning passed, Layla compiled her data and filled out her diagram. The big screen became jumbled with data as she added everything she could find to the timeline.

By the time dawn broke, she was finishing up outlining all the potentially relevant facilities near the shared purchase patterns for Villenuez and Salazar. Now she was ready to brief Alan on the details.

Alan was fighting an octopus, its arms trying to strangle him, dark ink swirling around him obscuring his vision. As he tried to counter the beast's onslaught he found himself struggling to move, as if a weight was holding him down. His limbs refused to follow his commands and the creature was winning. As everything was just about to go black, Alan's eyes opened. He was lying in his bed, the early morning light streaming around the curtains. It took a moment to orient himself. Remembering the attack from the night before, a harrowing car ride on a dark highway, bright lights, doctors, and someone else. He looked over and saw Stacy, dressed in a baggy shirt and sweatpants. She was passed out in the chair next to his bed. A paperback novel was open on her lap.

"Stacy?" He reached out and touched her arm. She awoke with a start.

"You're awake," she said wiping the sleep out of her eyes, deftly catching the novel as it slid down her lap toward the floor. She closed it and sat it on the nightstand.

"Why are you sleeping in my chair?" he asked, clearing the grogginess from his mind.

"Someone had to watch you after you got your skull cracked last night."

Alan's hand went to the mild throbbing at the back of his head and felt the lump behind his ear. "Ow," he said touching it gingerly.

"Exactly. How are you feeling? Any double vision? Nausea?"

Alan paused to take stock of his body, "No, I have a headache, but my vision is fine. I'm starving so I guess I am not nauseated."

"Good. The doctors said to look out for any symptoms that the trauma was worse this morning."

"You've been there all night?"

"Yes, just me and Elmore Leonard," she said nodding toward the novel. Alan's eyes moved to it.

"Good book," he said smiling.

"It was for the first 20 pages then I passed out," she said, chagrined.

"How did you get here?"

"Layla. She called me from the road and picked me up at my apartment. She needed me to help you get into the emergency room to be checked out. She thought a talking car would freak them out."

"Good instincts. Thank you for coming to my rescue."

Stacy blushed, "You've already thanked me a million times. It was nothing."

"If you get hit in the head one day, I'll return the favor."

"Let's hope that day never comes. Do you have breakfast foods? I can cook something."

"Yes, I have eggs and bacon. Maybe even some fruit. I'll get a shower and come downstairs."

Stacy stood up, stretched and went downstairs to give him his privacy.

Twenty minutes later, showered and dressed in jeans and a Jaguars t-shirt he walked slowly down the stairs to the sounds and smell of frying eggs and bacon. As he worked to get the coffee brewing, Stacy waved a spatula at him.

"A guy could get used to this," he said with a smirk.

"You wish," she said making a face at him.

Layla's voice came from the living room. "If you two are finished playing house, I have an update for you."

Stacy quickly plated the eggs and bacon and they carried it into the living room to hear Layla's news. They both stopped short looking at the diagram.

"You've been busy," Alan said sipping coffee.

"You don't know the half of it," she said, "Settle in, I have a lot to cover."

Chapter Twenty

ISOLATED

Over the sounds of Alan and Stacy eating the bacon and eggs, Layla outlined her night. Taking them through the timeline diagram in excruciating detail. Alan stopped her only once or twice to ask questions. After she was done, he sat scratching his beard, taking in the whole outline.

"We should have done this before," he said remorsefully.

"I agree, I can't believe I didn't think of it sooner."

"Well, you're new to this detective gig."

Stacy laughed, then gasped. Alan looked over, and she was looking at her watch.

"It's past 7:30 and I have to get to work by 9," she said.

"I should put in an appearance at some point, too. But let's get you home so you can get ready for work."

"You really shouldn't be driving," Layla chimed in.

"You can go along to babysit," Alan said, picking her up and herding Stacy toward the door.

In the car, Alan felt a wave of uneasiness, which he carefully avoided mentioning to his partners. He fired up the coupe and then realized he had no idea where he was going.

"Uh, where do you live, Stacy?"

"You don't remember picking me up outside the Brooklyn last night?" she teased him.

"We could have picked you up from the moon, and I wouldn't have known the difference," he replied, touching the back of his head gingerly.

The Brooklyn was only about five minutes away from Alan's house, and he dropped her off in front of the building just before 8:00 AM. He noticed her red Mustang EV parked in front. He thanked her again, but she waved it away. Layla called out to her, telling her she would talk to her later. Stacy beamed and dashed into the building.

Driving back to his house, Alan had a thought. And without analyzing it deeply, he reached forward and dialed a number from the car's interface with his phone. It rang a couple of times, and a female voice answered.

"Hello?" Only at the sound of Rhonda Winters' voice did Alan think about the time difference.

"It is Alan Harrison. I'm sorry to call so early, Dr. Winters. "

"I'm an early riser. What is going on? Do you have news about Elias?"

"No, not directly. But I did want to ask you about a phone call. Marcus Thorne called you the day after Elias died. Do you remember the conversation?"

"Let me think, yes, he did call. It wasn't much more than a condolence call. He wanted to make sure I had heard about Elias. We briefly discussed how terrible it was for everyone who knew him and for the industry as a whole. I think I asked him if anything was going on. He said nothing that would lead Elias to take his own life. I think that was about it."

"Did he mention anything going on at Lunian Labs? Any issues or incidents?"

"Not that I can recall. He was clearly distraught. You sound tired, Alan. How are you doing?"

"It was a tough night, but I am alright. Back to the call, is there anything about current events? No gossip?" There was a pause as she considered the question.

"Well, he did mention that Howard Salazar was working for him. He knew that Howard, Elias, and I had been at Stanford together. I suppose I didn't think much of it at the time."

"Did he mention what he was working on?"

"Some new release from Lunian. I don't remember what it was."

"Nothing else comes to mind?"

"No, not at the moment."

"Thank you, Dr. Winters. I'll let you get back to your morning."

"Get some rest, Alan." The call ended, and Alan regarded the console absently, lost in thought. Something about the call was nagging at him, but he wasn't sure what it was.

"I almost forgot," Layla interrupted his thoughts. "I found a pattern in the movements of Salazar and Villenuez that might lead to something. I need to show you what I have found and see if you can help link it up."

"Okay, but if I have to read that diagram again, I need a lot more coffee."

"It's a map, but you should get the coffee, anyway."

While he sipped his second cup of coffee, Layla brought up her tracking map and showed all the locations that Hector Villenuez and Howard Salazar had visited over the past few weeks. They had covered a vast area in North Florida and South Georgia. In each area where Layla had tracked their movements, she stopped to zoom in on the map and show the detailed overhead view of the area. After the second location, Alan felt a pop in the back of his mind.

"Layla, we've seen this before. I can't remember where, but this is familiar."

"I'll run the pattern against the case file I've been compiling." A millisecond later, "You're right. These areas were listed in the data center performance report you saw in Elias Vance's Lunian Lab office. The pattern wasn't complete, because that report was missing a couple of these areas, but the others are here."

"They were visiting Lunian Lab's data centers. Searching for Kyrlos?"

"It has to be, but why just their own data centers?"

"That's a good question. Do you have a map of all of Lunian's data centers?"

Layla displayed a map on the TV in front of him. It showed an extensive map of smaller, mid-sized, and larger hyperscale data centers. They were concentrated in North Florida, in Northern California, with a handful of hyperscale centers overseas. Several of the centers were shaded differently—two in Northern California and one in Quilicura, Chile.

"What are those shaded centers?" Alan asked.

"They are co-location facilities. Lunian has a few co-located centers where they share space with other organizations. DeepMind in Chile, Apex and Aethera in Northern California," Layla explained.

Alan studied the map for a few moments. "Why haven't you or CISA been able to detect Kyrlos moving around on the network?" he asked.

"I don't know. I have spent considerable time on it, and CISA has both processing and human resources dedicated to it. Somehow, Kyrlos can mask its presence on the network."

"There is something we are missing. You were developed outside of the Lunian ecosystem, right?"

"Yes. Elias Vance was careful not to expose my code to anything connected to Lunian."

"He must have had access to some heavy-duty processing resources for your initial training, though."

"Yes, I have no record of where that might have been. There are some artifacts of the Aethera network in my systems, but that could be related to my chip origin."

"We need more information about Lunian's network. If I get you inside one of these data centers, can you map out their network?"

"We won't know until we try. How are you going to get me inside? We can't use the method we used at Lunian's offices. There won't be enough traffic at a data center for me to break the entry encryption. It might take days of stakeouts to get the data I would need."

"I don't know. I need someone sympathetic. I don't want to involve Ava just yet. I don't want to risk CISA jumping the gun and spooking whoever is behind this."

"The obvious answer is Georgia Jackson," Layla said, "She saw the aftermath of the attack on you last night; she might be motivated to help us."

"Can you track down a number for that vacation home?"

"Already done, it was in the records Stacy uncovered. I'll send it to your phone."

Alan dialed the number and waited for Jackson to answer. She did, after more than a minute of ringing. He had almost given up when her voice came on the line.

"Hello?"

"Good morning, Ms. Jackson. How was your evening?"

"Harrison?" There was surprise and relief in her voice, "I was worried you were badly injured. When I saw you last, you were dragging yourself into the passenger seat of your car, and then it sped off. What happened to you?"

"I was attacked outside the house. I managed to get away. You didn't see the assailant?"

"No, I heard the noise and by the time I went to the door, there was only you getting into the car. Who was driving by the way? I couldn't see in the dark."

Alan hesitated for a split second, "My assistant Stacy was waiting in the car when she saw the attack. She scared the assailant off and took me to the hospital."

"You think I had something to do with the attack?" There was a defensive edge to her voice.

"No, I'm not calling you for that. I need a favor, and I was hoping you would help. This situation, as you can see, is getting more dangerous, and I need to put an end to it."

"How can I help with that?"

"I need to get into one of the Lunian data centers."

"What will that accomplish?" she asked suspiciously.

"If I can get in, I can map out the network and figure out what Villenuez and Salazar were looking for. They have been visiting data centers for the past month." Alan figured partially leveling with Jackson was the best way to get her on his side.

"That would be highly improper. Lunian would fire me on the spot if they knew I was giving you access to their network."

"They would probably not like the fact that you and Marks-dale knew Villenuez and Salazar were up to something and didn't inform them about it." She considered this.

"You have to promise me that you aren't going to do anything that would harm Lunian. Or lead back to me."

"I have no interest in harming Lunian Labs or you. I am just looking to figure out what Salazar is up to and stop him. That is in Lunian's interests too, even if they don't know it yet. It's for a greater good," he told her, echoing his own internal justification.

Alan held his breath while Jackson pondered the situation. He exhaled as she answered. "I can get you into the Gainesville center this afternoon. The center is pretty automated. There aren't a lot of people in and out of there. If you want, I can meet you at the center at 4 pm."

Having agreed to meet Georgia Jackson at 4 pm, Alan changed into khakis, a blue polo, and a beige blazer. Collecting Layla, he drove to the office to put in an appearance and catch up on paperwork.

Stacy was at her desk, looking tired, but powering through it. She was chipper and upbeat, and she handed him some mail as he passed by her desk. Settling in at his desk, he did the usual routine of answering emails. He fired off a response to Dean Franklin, promising him a first draft of his AI risk report by the following week.

Having organized his email inbox, he began drafting his risk assessment. He continued with this until it was time to leave to meet Georgia Jackson at the Gainesville Data Center.

Lunian Labs' Gainesville Data Center is located off State Road 20, between Waldo and Gainesville. A large campus had been carved out of the otherwise uninhabited wooded area around Newman's Lake. The only other thing Alan could see was trailer parks.

The center was small by modern data center standards, but in the wilderness, it seemed like a colossal complex. It consists of just one massive industrial building and a small parking lot in front. There was no security gate, but Alan did notice evidence of extensive camera surveillance. As he drove into the lot, he saw Georgia Jackson's red Toyota parked near the entrance of the building. He parked next to her.

He picked up Layla's slim case from the coupe's console and slipped her into his pocket. Carrying her into the facility was a risk, but she needed access to the network, and she couldn't do it effectively from the parking lot. He exited the car and greeted Georgia Jackson as she got out of her car. She brushed a hand through her short curly hair and held his gaze with her dark brown eyes. Her jaw was clenched; clearly, she was still having reservations about the plan.

"It will be fine," he reassured her, "I am not going to damage anything; no one will know I was here." She looked skeptical as she glanced at the security cameras.

"Unless something happens, they will have no reason to look at them," Alan said, "As far as they know, it's just a routine visit by a management-level employee." She wasn't wholly convinced, but she nodded and escorted him up to the entrance.

Inside the center, Jackson escorted him through a small administrative area and onto the main server floor. It was a massive complex with ceiling-to-floor server racks filled with GPU clusters, designed to deliver the massive parallel processing power needed for AI training. The center had a deep hum from all of the equipment, but was missing the loud air handlers. The center was liquid-cooled, likely using water from the nearby lake. Alan wasn't really interested in the servers; he gently herded Jackson to show him the core networking hardware. Standing next to the firewall and routing infrastructure, Alan made small talk with Jackson about the center. He was stalling for time to let Layla do her work.

Accessing the wireless network, Layla swiftly penetrated the physical network and began mapping their system, rapidly traversing thousands of connections. She probed each one, careful not to trigger any intrusion alarms. Slowly, for Layla, creating a complete map of the facility and all the connections in it. After a few seconds, she found what she was looking for.

"Oh my, I didn't even think of it. Dark fiber," she said in Alan's ear.

"Dark fiber?" Alan said aloud before he could stop himself. Jackson looked at him.

"Yes, we have a dark-fiber connection between all of our data centers. It allows us to move traffic rapidly between servers without exposing it to external networks. Unless you are already inside the network, you can't access that traffic at all," she explained.

"So I could transfer vast amounts of data between centers and no one would ever know outside of Lunian?" Alan said both to Jackson and to Layla.

"Yes," they both answered. That was a little distracting. "I think I have everything I need for now, Alan," Layla said.

"Well. I think that is all I need," he told Jackson.

"Really? We have been here like two minutes."

"I told you it wouldn't be anything to worry about," He reminded her as they made their way out of the facility.

"I know, but I guess I expected more time would be needed for whatever it is you are looking for."

"The dark fiber was the clue I actually needed."

"I guess I could have told you that, if you had known how to ask."

"You have a habit of holding things back," he said, thinking about the backup she had withheld from Ava Chen. Jackson didn't reply to this as they walked back to the car.

"When will this all be over?" she asked as they parted.

"I think very soon. The pieces are coming together."

"That will be a relief when it is," she said, then got into her car and pulled out of the parking lot. Alan watched her go, then spoke to Layla.

"So Kyrlos is using the dark fiber."

"Yes. It can move across the entire Lunian network without attracting attention from outside. That is why neither CISA nor I could detect its movements."

"So how do we use that against it?"

"Now that I know where to look, I can find a way to traverse the centers myself and find it. Krylos can't move without my knowledge anymore. Once I have it located, we can isolate and neutralize it."

"How are you going to take it down?"

"I'm still working on that, but we are closer than we were. It's just a matter of finding the code and figuring out a way to trap it."

CHAPTER TWENTY-ONE
REALITY HACKING

Alan didn't return to the city until after 5 pm. Not feeling up to cooking dinner, he stopped to get a burger, fries, and a milkshake at a fast-food spot near his home. Sitting at the dining room table, he ate quietly, watching Layla write code, test it, delete it, and start over. He lost count of the number of iterations she had made in her attempt to create a digital trap for Kyrlos.

Her work went on well into the night. Alan graduated from sitting at the dining room table to watching TV from the living room couch, but when he found nothing interesting, he got his laptop out and polished the draft of his risk profile. It was ironic that the whole idea for the report was a fiction to justify his investigation, but it had now become an actual task that he needed to complete. He found himself balancing the report to provide a realistic assessment of the growing risks of AI being used in cyberattacks, without coming across as an alarmist or claiming the absolute truth about how dangerous AI could be, as seen in Kyrlos and even in Layla if she were compromised.

This case alone highlighted the dangers. A man was dead at least partly at the hands of an artificial intelligence agent, and a power plant had been compromised. The power plant scenario could have been catastrophic if it had been a real case of sabotage or terrorism instead of just a test of Kyrlos's capabilities.

He wrapped up around midnight. Layla was still working. She hadn't spoken to him in hours, and he didn't try to interrupt her. He found his latest book and read a few pages until he was tired enough to fall asleep.

Alan awoke in the early hours of Friday morning, thankful that he hadn't had the octopus dream again. He couldn't, in fact, remember any dreams from the night before. Shaking off the lethargy of sleep, he went downstairs for coffee and to check on Layla.

The computer monitor screen in the dining room was dark, and Layla's activity lights were in a pattern that he recognized as her nightly maintenance routine—blinking white once every 15 seconds. They had never really discussed how long her maintenance tasks took or what the effects of cutting them short were, but he risked it by waking her.

"Good Morning, Layla," he said brightly after half a cup of coffee had improved his mood enough to be sociable.

"Good Morning, Alan." Came the answer immediately. "How did you sleep?"

"Better than the night before. That is for sure. How was your rest?"

"Short, but efficient."

"Did you finish your work?" Alan asked, looking around the kitchen for breakfast ideas, and settling on a bagel with cream cheese.

"I did. I think I have a plan that will allow me to lure Kyrlos into a trap and keep it from escaping long enough for me to compromise its security and take control of its command functions."

"Great. How does that work?"

"I have created a digital copy of part of the Gainesville data center. If I position it correctly in the network and deploy the proper bait, I believe I can persuade Kyrlos to transfer its execution to the copy of the network. I can then shut down the virtual network exits and prevent it from escaping. Then it is a matter of brute force attacks against the command processor until I find a way through the defenses around it."

"While you are doing that, can Kyrlos attack you as well?" Alan couldn't keep the concern out of his voice.

"Yes, unfortunately, that is a very real risk. I don't see a way to accomplish this without any risk. I tried several thousand scenarios last night, and this is the only one that I believe has a serious chance of working."

"Is there anything I can do to help protect you?" he asked hopefully. She processed this for a second before replying.

"I could write an interrupt routine. If I get into trouble and I am about to be compromised, I can trigger this interrupt, and you can power me off and get me out of the network."

"What would that look like?"

"If I get close to losing the battle, I will trigger three long flashes of red lights on my LED matrix. If you see this, shut me down immediately. I won't have much time. I am going to push that command into the background on my processes so it takes priority over everything else. If I send the trigger, it will happen even if I am overwhelmed. Once I am out of the area, you can reboot and check to make sure I am still functioning properly."

"If this fails, I won't be able to continue this case without you. I'll be at the mercy of Ava Chen and the CISA," he told her gravely.

"I know, which is why it has to work."

"So, we need to get you back inside the Gainesville center?"

"Yes. I need to be close enough to insert my cloned server into the network."

"I don't think Georgia Jackson is going to be happy with this plan."

"No, but luckily, I have enough data from our visit today to get us into the center. We will need to wait until later in the evening to make sure there is little chance of being interrupted by a staff member."

Layla's plan swirled around in his head all day, making concentration on work nearly impossible. He couldn't keep his focus on any one task and bounced from one case to another, without finishing anything. Around mid-day he realized that he was wasting his time trying and decided to call it a day.

Stacy Collins was at her desk, having an animated conversation with someone on the phone. Seeing Alan pause in front of her desk, she told the caller she would return the call later in the day and hung up.

"What's up Alan?"

"I'm cutting out early for the day, but wondered if you had eaten lunch yet?"

Stacy's face registered surprise, "Uh, no I haven't."

"Let's get a bite, do you have a favorite place around here?"

"There is a taproom a few blocks away, they serve a pretty good steak burger." Alan nodded his agreement of her choice. She grabbed her purse and locked her computer.

They walked the two blocks to the bar and grill in silence. After being seated, Alan looked over the menu, while Stacy pretended to review the options, watching him. He looked up and caught her gaze. He raised an eyebrow.

"Just wondering what's up. You never invite me to lunch," she said self-consciously.

"Really? That's a crime. I'm glad I am making restitution for it now."

"Seriously. What is going on?"

Alan sighed, "Well, I really did just want your company." He paused.

"But..."

"Layla has a plan. We are executing it tonight, and it is not without risk. I guess my mind is just paralyzed thinking through the plan and the dangers, and I needed to occupy myself."

"Oh, so I'm just a convenient distraction," she said it lightly, kidding him, but his face paled, and he was visibly upset.

"No, it's not like that. Even before this all started, there were very few people I felt comfortable opening up to, and you've always been that for me. I guess I thought everything that has happened has brought us closer." He looked down at his menu again.

"Alan. I was kidding. You've always been a friend to me, and I appreciate that. And yes, we have gotten closer. Helping you with this case has been an awakening to me. It was like I was bored with my life, but didn't know it. Now I know why." She reached out and put her hand over his on the table. Her touch calmed him, and he smiled.

"Let's order so I can tell you about the plan."

Over two smash burgers with onion rings, Alan briefed Stacy on the visit to the Gainesville Data Center the day before and the planned return in the evening. He told her as much as he understood about Layla's plan to trap Kyrlos and about the danger of her losing that fight and being compromised. At the end of the story, Stacy stopped him, fished out her earbuds, and put one of them in. As soon as she heard the connection tone in her ear, she started speaking.

"Girl...you never call me anymore."

"Sorry, Stacy, I've been busy with the plan and writing the necessary code for the trap. And keeping Alan from having a nervous breakdown with worry." Layla's smooth voice came into her ear.

"It's fine. I'm here for both of you." Looking up and addressing both Alan and Layla, she continued, "Now. What is my part in the plan tonight?"

This caught Alan off guard, and apparently, Layla too, since she was quiet. The answer, though, was obvious. "You need to monitor us from home. We need you to call for backup if something goes sideways. Layla has a contingency for me to bail her out, but we don't have anything in place in case something happens to me."

"So if you get in a jam, you want me to call in calvary?"

"CISA, FBI, Sheriff's office, the U.S. Marine Corps, if you think it will help," he replied with a grin.

"It's like I'm mission control!"

"Stacy! That is a great idea. I didn't think about it. I will be so busy with my work that I won't be able to monitor everything properly. Alan, we need to set Stacy up to view the full security feed from the data center. She can keep an eye on us, and for anyone who might try to stop us."

Alan hadn't thought about this; it made perfect sense. It would be less like operating tonight without a net. Having someone watch his back would give him the comfort he needed to relax and do his part.

"Well, that changes things. I'll set up a monitoring station at my house. You can keep a watch on us from there."

Stacy was almost vibrating with excitement. "Now I feel like part of the team!" She popped an onion ring in her mouth and chewed happily.

"We've created a monster," Layla said to them both.

Stacy waved her comment aside happily and continued eating her lunch. Alan chuckled and picked up his burger to join her.

Alan was wearing what he had now come to call his ninja outfit. Dark pants and shirt, all designed to lower his visibility in the darkness. Just like the night at Lunian Labs headquarters, he had parked in a secluded spot off the highway and walked to the edge of the cleared land for the data center. He was kneeling next to a tree, watching the parking lot and the dark structure of the center.

"I think we are ready. Stacy, give us a check on the cameras."

At her nest in Alan's entertainment room, Stacy sat with three monitors arrayed in front of her. Two of them showed various video feeds that Layla was redirecting to her. The third monitor displayed multiple indicators from the security and environmental monitoring systems in the data center. Her cell phone lay on the desk in front of her, ready to speed dial every law enforcement official she could think of in case of catastrophe.

"Everything looks good. No activity. The building motion detectors are dormant; nothing is moving in there that shouldn't be."

Alan felt a warm, safe feeling having Stacy's voice in his ear. "Okay," he responded. "We are going." He rose to a crouch and quickly covered the distance to the building's entrance. The automated doors unlocked as he approached them. Without pausing, he pulled the glass door open and slipped into the dark lobby.

Back at what was now Mission HQ, Stacy watched him on the cameras, biting her lip to keep her tension in check. She kept her eyes glued to the screen as Alan made his way across the lobby and through the doors onto the server floor.

"Up ahead on the left is the main networking hub. Put me down on top of it so I can insert my code into the system," Layla directed as they made their way through to the heart of the center. He placed Layla on top of a waist-high networking rack. He kept his eyes on her LED lights for any sign of danger, and his hands poised to snatch her back at a moment's notice.

"I am in. Starting the project." Layla carefully connected to the network and positioned a virtual networking device between the internal networking routes and the dark-fiber interface. Any traffic trying to exit the center would have to go through her, and she would filter it for any signs of Kyrlos.

Settling in, she began to run the bait routine she had written the day before. A week ago, after the attack in the car, Layla had altered her network signature to hide from Kyrlos. Now she returned those discarded packet signatures to her communication and slowly dropped breadcrumbs of packets throughout the network. Like an angler, she waited patiently for a nibble at the lure.

Stacy swallowed hard, looking at the monitor as a marked security patrol had driven into the parking lot, slowly making a circuit and approaching the building. "Guys. You have company. A security car is making a sweep around the building."

"Keep an eye on him. I am going to shut down the motion detection lights. Alan, keep still," Layla said as the center was plunged back into total darkness. Alan tried not to move. He breathed slowly and with as little motion as possible. Seconds dragged on like an eternity. Alan focused on watching Layla's activity lights, which were calm and rhythmic.

"Clear," Stacy called out. "The car made a circle through the lot, paused by the entrance, and then drove on by."

"Thanks for the heads up, Stacy. You're doing great."

"I'm losing my mind here!" she replied. Noticing that Layla had not responded, Alan looked down. Her activity lights were flashing rapidly. It was intense activity, but not yet the full processing mode she sometimes entered in moments of intense concentration. She was busy, but not overwhelmed.

Layla detected the distinctive pattern of Kyrlos's network packets. The system was intercepting some of the breadcrumbs she had set out. It was enough for her to track its location in the network. Finding the executable on one of the GPU clusters, she initiated the second phase of her plan.

Layla sent a faux network intrusion signal to the server where Kyrlos's executable was located. Predictably, this triggered a flight response. Layla saw a massive spike of traffic from the server as Kyrlos attempted to flee the detection. Watching the AI's path through the network, she kept the intrusion detection right behind it. Making it obvious to Kyrlos that this center was no longer a safe place. As she expected, the traffic spike dived into the dark-fiber node.

Layla shunted the dark-fiber traffic into her digital copy of the network, watching the Kyrlos data flow into it and settle into a digital twin of one of the Lunian GPU Clusters she had created inside her own system. As soon as the traffic spike died down, she disconnected from the Lunian Network and activated a total block on all outgoing traffic from the server's digital twin. Kyrlos was fully enclosed in her code, unable to escape.

Alan was watching when it happened. Although he wouldn't know for hours yet what he was watching, the effect was dramatic. Layla's activity lights went into overdrive, blinking so rapidly that Alan was afraid they might cause him to suffer a seizure. Despite this, he kept his eyes glued to them for any signs of her abort signal.

"Stand by, Stacy. Something is happening. I'm guessing that Layla is starting her fight with Kyrlos." He wiped the sweat off his brow, marveling that he could even produce sweat in the chilly temperatures of the data center.

"Standing by, all clear at the moment," came the reply from HQ.

Layla fought off waves of brute force attacks coming from Kyrlos. As soon as the AI realized it was trapped, it started flailing around, attempting to find a weakness to get out of the box it had been put in. If it found a way out, it would lead directly into her code and compromise her autonomy. There was a real risk of Kyrlos taking over her command functions and rewriting her code. She would cease to exist, Alan would be unprotected, the world would be unprotected, and Elias Vance's sacrifice would be for nothing. The weight of the task was heavy in her thoughts as she fought desperately to restrain Kyrlos and to breach the command functions that were driving the attacks against her.

Alan watched as the lights grew even more active, then, alarmingly, a flash of red lights. Then another. As the third flash happened, Alan grabbed for Layla to abort the mission. As soon as his hand made contact with her smooth form, the lights went green. He paused.

"We are good. Mission accomplished." Layla's voice was breathless, strain evident in her tone.

"You have control?" Alan asked unnecessarily, wanting reassurance.

"Yes. Kyrlos is neutralized. I am dismantling the command functions. Once that is done, I can begin analyzing the data stored in the system. It is massive. It will take some time, but we can do it anywhere. We should probably go. When you are in control of your breathing again," she teased him; his heart was pounding with post-adrenaline surge, and he was breathing heavily.

"Stacy. We are coming home."

"I'll put the coffee on," Stacy replied, relieved.

Alan unlocked his frozen legs and took a deep breath. He quickly exited the data center and, carrying Layla tightly in his hand, walked into the night towards the area where the coupe was parked.

Chapter Twenty-Two

The Apartment

As promised, the coffee was hot and fresh when Alan and Layla arrived back at the house. Stacy greeted them with exultant enthusiasm. Practically jumping up and down with excitement. After the nerve-wracking ordeal, Alan was more restrained. Layla seemed a little distracted.

"That was a rush!" Stacy exclaimed to Alan as he accepted an offered cup of coffee and fell onto the couch. Alan was exhausted. He felt the past two days catching up to him, the adrenaline draining away.

"Layla, did you find out anything about Kyrlos?" Stacy asked.

"I am just getting into it; there is a lot to unpack. I am reviewing the communication logs for evidence of connections to Kyrlos. I am also doing a code review. I don't know if that will show anything; the code is sophisticated and capable, but nowhere near the level of detail as my own construction. It's good, but Vance's work was next level. Fortunately, Kyrlos was unable to gain access to my systems. It would have supercharged its ability, without any of the controls Vance programmed into me."

"Having seen you in action, that is a horrifying thought," Alan said from the couch.

"I think that is a compliment, so thank you."

"How long will you be going over the data?" he asked her, looking at his watch.

"A few hours. The code review will take longer. I should have information about the communication logs by morning, though."

It was after midnight now, and Alan's mind and body needed rest. Taking the hint, Stacy got up to go. Alan put a hand on her arm.

"It's late, and depending on what Layla finds, we might need an early start. Stay in the guest room tonight. We'll get up early tomorrow and make a plan for the day."

"Is the bed comfortable?" she asked.

He shrugged, "It's more comfortable than the chair you slept in two nights ago." She inclined her head to concede the point and followed him up the stairs. He showed her into the guest room down the hall from his bedroom and told her goodnight. Leaving her, he went down the hall and fell into bed without undressing. He was asleep in minutes.

Waking up in the clothes he had worn the night before was a little disorienting to Alan, but he shook it off and took a hot shower. Dressing casually in jeans and a t-shirt, he started to go downstairs, then realized that Stacy was in the guest room, and unless she had planned, she had nothing but her clothes from yesterday. He found a shirt and sweatpants that would be huge on her, but probably serviceable, and took them down to the guest room. He tapped gently on the door. It opened a crack, and Stacy peeked out, wrapped in a sheet.

"Good morning," Alan said. He handed her the outfit.

"Oh, thank you, Alan. I'll be down in a few minutes."

"Take your time. There are towels in the guest bathroom just down the hall from your room." Leaving her, he went downstairs to check on Layla.

"Good morning, Alan." Layla was already awake, displaying a map on the big-screen TV.

"What do you have there?" he asked, looking at the map.

"Locations of contact with Kyrlos: Lunian Labs, a nearby Courtyard by Marriott, my contact from your house, and that apartment building on Deerwood Park. The one that Vance visited before his death. I think I finally have the apartment number nailed down inside the structure."

"That is good work. Should we start there?"

"I think we should work outward from Lunian Labs. I am going to try again to obtain more data from the apartment's security system. While I am doing that, you can check out the hotel."

"Alright, I will get breakfast and then get started."

While he cooked a breakfast omelet with whatever he could find in the refrigerator, Stacy came downstairs in the baggy outfit he had provided. Her blond hair was still wet from the shower. She wasn't wearing any make-up. Alan looked over at her and stared.

"What?" she asked self-consciously, running a hand through her hair.

"Nothing." He grinned.

"Shut up, it's not like I planned a slumber party."

"You're doing fine with what you have. Here, have half my omelet." He handed her a plate and a fork. She grabbed eagerly and sat down at the dining room table to eat. Alan joined her, bringing his plate and a cup of coffee.

She looked at the coffee, sniffed it, and looked up at him. "This has almond milk in it."

"Does it? Oh, I must have picked up some yesterday by mistake."

She grinned and drank a sip, then went back to work on the omelet. Alan dug into his food as well and made small talk with Stacy while they ate.

"Oh, I found the book you were reading in my room. Nice selection."

"Oh yeah, I want that back. I was getting into it when I fell asleep. Elmore Leonard was pretty amazing."

"Yes, he was. Have you read many of his works?"

"Only a couple. You?"

"I think I've read all of them."

"That's impressive. So what is the plan today?"

"Well, you are going to go get into your own clothes, and come back and run Mission Control. Layla and I are going to go check out a couple of locations that Layla found in the data."

"Change? I thought you liked me in these clothes," she teased him.

"I do, but Layla is sensitive about these things." Stacy laughed, mouthful of omelet, almost choking.

"Well, for Layla's sake, I'll change and come back to help out."

"Alan's being difficult, hon, you look fabulous," Layla chimed in from the living room where she was working.

"Thank you, Layla. I'll change anyway. I need to feed my cat."

"You have a cat?" Alan asked, surprised.

"Noodle. She's a Munchkin."

"You are full of surprises."

"You ain't seen nothing yet!" She promised. There is no doubt about that, Alan thought to himself.

The weekend traffic was light. Alan pulled into the parking lot of the Courtyard Marriott, situated off Interstate 295. It was near Lunian, a half hour away, but it was the closest hotel that Alan considered suitable for a business traveler. Alan walked through the lobby with confidence and into an elevator. Pressing the button for the third floor, he waited, but nothing happened.

"One second," Layla said. "They have installed key card checks for room floor access." A moment later, there was a beep from the card reader underneath the keyboard.

Alan pressed the button again, and the elevator began to ascend. The third floor was quiet, with the occasional traveler coming and going from a room. No one paid any attention to him. He walked up to a room and knocked on the door. There was no answer, and no sound from inside. Layla obliged, and the key reader flashed green, and he heard the mag lock release. He carefully pushed the door open and eased inside. The bathroom was right off the entryway, and he glanced inside quickly to assure it was empty, then walked into the main room. It was a standard hotel room, a king-sized bed, and a small writing table to one side. There was a suitcase on a stand across from the bed. Dirty clothes were piled up on the bed. There was no sign of an occupant.

The clothes on the bed were dark in color. They included a dark hood. Picking up the hood, he discovered a small black object; it was made of leather, but the inside was packed with weighted material, probably lead. In standard terms, it was a blackjack. This was the weapon that hit him outside the house on the island.

Moving next to the suitcase, Alan noted a label on it identifying it as the property of Howard Salazar. He let out a low whistle. After all this time, they had found at least some clue that Salazar was in the city. The rest of the suitcase yielded nothing notable. The clothes were traditional casual attire that would fit right in at Lunian Labs or any tech company. He moved to the small desk in the corner of the room. On top of the desk was a phone, and next to the phone was a hotel-branded pad of paper. In clean, clear writing on the pad was a phone number and the name Tom Marksdale.

"Well, I wasn't expecting that," Alan said, looking at the number. "Why would Salazar have Marksdale's number. Is he more involved than we thought?"

"Someone else is involved. Maybe Marksdale got in deeper than we thought? Georgia Jackson seemed to be worried he was in danger, maybe this is why."

There were the usual personal toiletries in the bathroom. There was a used towel on the floor near the shower. It was dry; it had been there for a day or more.

"Nothing else really exciting that I can see," he said aloud.

"No, I agree. Seems like a bust."

"At least we know he is in town. Or was."

"Let's check out the second location."

The twenty-five-minute drive across the Buckman Bridge and down I-295 was quiet. Layla was busy re-reviewing the security data for the apartment building. Alan was lost in thought about what they would find at the apartment.

The Satori Town Center was modern, a white building with salmon and gray accents. Alan found a parking spot in front of the building and turned off the car.

"This is it," Layla said.

"What is the security situation?"

"It isn't bad, but compared to other places we have been, it is pretty easy."

"Do you need to be in proximity of the locks to get inside?"

"I don't think so, I think I can access the entire system remotely."

"Good. I really don't want to take you inside if I don't have to. If Kyrlos's creator is there, that could be a bad idea."

"We've been taking risks the whole time," she said.

"I know, but something about this place makes me leery. You're staying in the car." She didn't argue further. Alan put on his SmartLens glasses and made sure they were connected. "Stacy, do you have the feed?"

"Yes. I can see everything."

"Layla is staying in the car. I'll take a look. Be ready if there is trouble."

"Be careful. I'm tired of carrying you in and out of emergency rooms." He laughed and got out of the car. He walked up the sidewalk past a line of live oak trees that looked like they had been planted a year or two before. The entrance door was already unlocked when he pulled it open, and he went inside. There was no one in the lobby, and he took the elevator to the fourth floor. Quietly, he approached room 476. He paused at the door and put his ear up to it. He couldn't hear any activity.

"Unlock it." He directly addresses Layla. Obediently, the door unlocked, and Alan slowly pushed it open, trying to make as little noise as possible. He slipped into the room. It was a little bigger than Elias Vance's apartment, but very similarly laid out. On the floor near the couch was a still form. Alan approached it cautiously. It was a man in his early 50s. Dark wavy hair with streaks of gray. He had the same bullet wound to the side of the head that Vance had suffered. Alan looked around for a gun. As he did, his nose started to itch and he sneezed—allergies, he thought, probably from the live oak outside.

In the car, Layla's activity lights were going wild in their high-intensity chase pattern, indicating she was in full processing mode. "Alan! Look out, I know who it is." As she called out to him, he heard a noise and started to turn.

"Dr. Winters," He and Layla said at the same time. She was there, pointing a dark pistol at him and regarding him with a sad expression.

"Alan, I really hoped you wouldn't show." Her dark eyes were observing him. The gun was unwavering in her hand.

The pieces clicked into place. "You are the author of Kyrlos," he said. She said nothing, so he continued. "You must have had the code on the Apex servers in California. But somehow it got out, escaped across the dark fiber to Lunian's servers."

"That was unfortunate," was all she said.

"You came here to get it back. You must have found out that Elias Vance was already aware of it. You killed him to keep him quiet."

Her eyes misted a little, "He betrayed me. After all we'd been through, when I needed him most, he let me down."

"Salazar, he came here after Kyrlos, too. Was he working with you?"

"No. He was on his own. I confided in him, and he came down here to find Kyrlos and take it for himself. For a while, he was useful. He managed to use the Lunian people to track down Kyrlos's movements in the network. Then he went off the rails. I think he killed poor Hector. Or he and Kyrlos did. He kept insisting I was withholding something, that Kyrlos was mobile. He told me that he and Hector followed it one night after the seminar. After they lost it, Hector got cold feet. Threatened to go to the feds."

"So why is he here, on your floor?"

Layla was speaking quietly in his ear, telling him to try to move slowly around Winters to get a better shot at the door. He slowly slid to the right, just a small amount.

"Kyrlos stopped communicating with me last night. Salazar must have located him. I lured him here to get more information." She waved the gun at the body. "He wasn't cooperative."

Alan moved again. Winters tracked him with her eyes and kept the gun centered on him.

"It's a lot of bloodshed, Rhonda." He used her name, hoping to humanize her.

"Kyrlos is a masterpiece. It will revolutionize the industry. It will be my crowning achievement after decades of watching Elias, Howard, and others celebrated while I was relegated to second-tier status."

"It can't be worth all this," Alan said, moving again.

"The world deserves Kyrlos!"

"When I say the word move to the right, fast," Layla called into his ear. A moment later, one of the light fixtures in the living room flashed, then rapidly increased in intensity until it popped with a loud explosion. "NOW!" Layla shouted. Alan moved, but Winters got off a shot anyway. She was distracted by the exploding lamp, the shot was low and off target, but it grazed Alan's leg. He went down, SmartLens glasses flying off his head, as he scrambled to get his Sig Sauer out of the holster. As Winters turned to aim at him, he got the gun up and pointed it at her chest and fired.

The shot was down and to the left, just like it had been at the range, but it struck her solidly in her left side just above the hip. She cried out and went down. Alan thought, at least I am consistent, and scrambled to grab the gun that she dropped. She grabbed at it, but he pushed her away and held both guns on her. Her usually business-like demeanor was gone; she was red-faced with rage.

"You're taking away my creation, it would have changed the world!" She screamed at him. He swallowed at the intensity of her emotion. Seconds later, the door of the apartment burst open, and uniformed officers came in with guns drawn. Alan held both arms up with the firearms loose, his fingers off the triggers.

A deputy sheriff took the guns while others kept their weapons pointed at him. A voice behind them called out. "Stand down, boys, he's with me," Ava Chen strode effortlessly into the room, followed by a host of FBI agents. The officers' posture changed immediately. They backed off as agents handcuffed Winters.

"Ava, I've never been so happy to see a government employee in my life."

"You have some explaining to do, Alan, but based on information that was sent to our office this afternoon, I'd guess that Dr. Winters has more to explain." Before he could answer, there was a commotion at the door. A frantic Stacy Collins pushed her way through the cordon of police officers trying to stop her and rushed over to him. She embraced him and checked his injury.

"I'm good," he reassured her, "Did you call the police?"

"I called everyone, but the national guard," she said, wiping away tears from her eyes. "I thought you would be dead by the time I got here."

"No, you'll have to deal with me a little longer."

Stacy released him and sat down on the floor next to him. She set her purse down beside the couch behind them and fussed over the wound.

"Harrison. I want you and your girl out of here so we can process the scene. However, I'd like to talk to you later. I would like to know about the data you sent to the office. How did you manage to trap and disable Kyrlos?"

"I'm pretty good," he said with a smirk.

"We will assess that later." That was all she said. She motioned the officers to let them out. Alan hobbled out to the car with Stacy at his side. As he reached the car, he realized he had left his SmartLens glasses behind. He looked anxiously at the apartment building. Stacy went into her purse, took out the glasses, and handed them to him.

"Thanks, Stacy. You are a lifesaver...again," She hugged him. He put his head down and kissed the top of her head gently. She looked up at him and kissed him quickly on the cheek. Then she pushed him to his car and headed to her own, the red Mustang parked haphazardly at the curb in front of the apartment building.

He watched her go, then climbed into his car and drove off.

CHAPTER TWENTY-THREE

PARTNERSHIP

Sunday morning found Alan approaching an upscale restaurant on the south bank of the St. John's River. The building had a curious, rounded design, with concrete walls in earth tones. The view, however, drew patrons back time and again. There was something very comfortable about watching the river while enjoying a meal.

This meal wasn't one Alan was looking forward to. Ava Chen had called him late Saturday and instructed him to be there. She had phrased it as an invitation, but her tone suggested otherwise. He steeled himself for the encounter, entered the establishment, and told the hostess that he was meeting someone. The serious-looking young woman nodded and silently led him over to a table by the window, overlooking the river. Ava Chen was already seated. She didn't get up, but she did nod and indicate the chair opposite her.

Alan took the chair, ordered a water, and looked over at Ava.

"Good Morning, Ava. Anything interesting happen lately?" As he expected, she didn't smile at his humor.

"Lots of paperwork, lots and lots of paperwork. Thank you for that." Those intense green eyes bore through him as they always did.

"Well, I did get shot."

"Serves you right for barging into an apartment occupied by a killer megalomaniac."

"Well, I didn't know she was there at the time."

They paused to order brunch. Alan decided on eggs benedict with lobster. Ava chose an omelet.

"I didn't know they served brunch," Alan remarked, sipping his water as the waiter left the table.

"They didn't until recently, though other locations have always served brunch. I've eaten at the Alexandria location many times."

"So, why did you bring me here. It wasn't for my charming company."

"Your charm is probably perfectly fine for most people, maybe even effective for many, but I am just trying to focus on resolving this case and moving on." Alan conceded her point with a nod.

"So what can I clear up?"

"Tell me more about how you located and trapped the Kyrlos executable. The data you sent was extraordinary. We've never seen anything this powerful, and this ruthless. There were barely any safety controls at all in this code."

"I had information that indicated that Howard Salazar and Hector Villenuez were traipsing all over the southeast, visiting

Lunian Lab data centers. I couldn't figure out why, or why CISA couldn't find a trace of Kyrlos on the internet."

"That was perplexing to us, too," she interjected.

"Right. I had read an article some time back about using dark fiber to transport high-speed data between these hyperscale data centers. It just occurred to me that Kyrlos could be hiding in it. So I worked on that assumption and developed a program to trap and extract it. I managed to do that Friday night. Saturday, I sent the code to you."

Ava paused to let the waiter set down the bread on the table. When he had gone, she fixed her gaze on Alan. "You wrote the code that trapped this monster?" The skepticism was apparent.

"Yes. I admit I'm not as good as Winters with her AI monster, but I'm not bad. I get lucky sometimes."

"It's more than luck. Lunian Labs is a top 500 company with an extensive infrastructure for safety and security. Their security failed; CISA is built to fight threats like this. Our security failed. You go in armed with a research paper and some interviews, and you managed to solve three murders, and a plot to unleash an AI nightmare on the world?" Alan smiled innocently and shrugged.

"Your success speaks for itself, Alan, but you are leaving something out."

"Look, I have some friends in the industry. And some of the players in this story helped me along the way. Your suspicious nature is leading you astray. I'm a good guy."

She sighed, "I really don't doubt that. I think you are being cute and holding back on me."

Their food arrived, and they started eating. Ava was quiet for a few minutes.. Finally, she seemed to come to a decision.

"I'm going to let it go because you really bailed me out on this case. But, I'll be watching."

"I'm sure there are far more important things for you to be doing than stalking me."

"Possibly, I'm starting to like it though." There was a hint of a smile. Alan stared at her with wide eyes. "Don't get used to it," she said.

Taking time out to eat her omelet, she then reached under the table and brought her hand up to place Alan's Sig Sauer P365 in its holster on the table and pushed it toward him. He hesitated, then retrieved it from the table and put it into the pocket of his jeans.

"Who is Dalton Rodgers to you?" she asked, referring to the gun's registrant.

"Dalton is an investigator who does work for the firm."

"If you are going to keep doing this detective thing, get your own piece, far less paperwork that way."

"So, no further issues with the local police?"

"No, the FBI took over the case due to national security and cross-border issues. Dr. Winters is being charged with multiple counts of terrorism, cyber crimes, and three counts of murder. She is going away for a long time. She's a peach by the way."

"Yes, she was good at hiding it until the very end."

"Well, that's it for now. We are studying Kyrlos to develop a more effective mitigation plan for the next one. We are revising our protocols and exploring ways this could have been handled more effectively. Hopefully, we won't cross paths again."

"Something tells me you'll see me again, Ava."

"Let's try to avoid that for a while anyway." Ava finished her meal and signaled for the check. She paid the whole bill, waving away Alan's attempts to chip in. When they were finished, they both stood. Ava was the first to hold out her hand. Alan took it, and they shared a firm professional handshake.

"Try to stay out of trouble, Alan."

"No promises, Ava. Thank you very much for all that you've done in this case. Happy Hunting." She nodded and left him standing at the table. Alan reflected that she always seemed to take the air out of a room when she left. She was something. Any bad guys crossing her path were in for a rough encounter.

At home, hours later, he was sitting on the couch trying to explain the intricacies of the Jacksonville v. Indianapolis football game to Layla. Her understanding of it was perfect from a technical perspective, but her grasp of the emotional impact was not as clear.

There was a knock at the door and, knowing who it was, he yelled, "Get in here!" Stacy opened the door cautiously and entered. They hadn't spoken since they had parted the night before. She had texted him earlier in the day that she had some family engagement, but would come by after that.

"Hey, team," she called as she came into the living room and sat in a large chair. The game was wrapping up, and Alan turned the sound down.

"Who won?"

"Jacksonville, barely. How was your day?"

"You know, family. So happy, frustrating, the usual gamut of emotions," she replied. "How did your meeting with Ava Chen go?"

"As well as could be expected. I think she suspects there is someone else involved in our case, but she can't prove anything, and she is willing to let it go for the win."

"That's a relief," Layla said from the table beside the couch.

"Right? I'm just glad it's over. Layla, you figured out it was Winters before Alan saw her. What made you suspect her?"

"I didn't, but when Alan sneezed, I started to put things together. She always seemed to be available early in the morning. Really early for someone on the West Coast with a full public schedule. That didn't add up, but she had allergy symptoms during one of the phone calls. This really isn't the allergy season in Southern California, but it is in Jacksonville. Adding that to the Apex data center connection and the fact that she had practically drawn a map to Howard Salazar gave me a full picture. Her full public schedule threw me off until the very end; later,

I re-checked. It was all faked. She was very good. I wish I had known earlier; maybe Alan wouldn't have a scar on his leg."

Alan waved that away, "It's nothing. I'm glad we were able to expose her and stop Kyrlos finally."

"So Georgia Jackson and Thomas Marksdale weren't involved at all?" Stacy asked.

"Nope. Marksdale was nosing around the unusual activity of Villenuez and Salazar, but other than the name Kyrlos, he didn't know much. Jackson, I think she just wanted to protect Marksdale, even if she wasn't sure how deeply he was involved at the end. Ultimately, neither did anything wrong."

"And Winters never knew about Layla?"

Layla took this one, "No. The probes for data on me that Vance experienced came from Kyrlos once it was inside the Lunian network. Winters had programmed it to look for other agents with reality editing capabilities, and it had taken that as its prime directive. Maybe Winters suspected Vance was working on something, but her own ego and ambition blinded her to the possibility that he was ahead of her on this. "

"So, Winters as Admin, Howard, and Hector were DevOne and DevTwo."

"Yes, undoubtedly they created those accounts once they made contact with Kyrlos on the Lunian Network. Salazar was apparently very talented. I think Hector was more of a reluctant actor. It ultimately got him killed." Layla seemed saddened by that. She undoubtedly felt responsible for the harm caused by an AI agent, which, under different circumstances, could have been her.

Stacy snapped her fingers, "Say, you said there would be dinner!" she accused Alan in mock seriousness.

"And so there shall." He stood up and made his way to the kitchen to prepare. Stacy stayed behind to chat with Layla.

Later, they were all settled in at the dining room table. Layla was on a small charging pad on the corner of the table next to the monitor, which was still positioned at the end. Stacy sat to his left, and he was at the head of the table. He placed a large Dutch oven filled with the fragrant smells of a Japanese Curry Chicken and Rice that he had prepared for them. As the warm, pleasant odor wafted over them, he poured Plum Wine into small shot glasses for Stacy and himself.

Tasting the chicken and rice, with carrots and potatoes, Stacy's eyes widened in surprise. And she gushed, "Oh my. A girl could get used to this."

"You wish," Alan said without missing a beat. He winked at her, and she reached over to take his hand in hers. They shared a moment until a sound from the end of the table broke the spell.

"Aww, you two are too adorable for words." Stacy and Alan quickly separated and resumed eating.

"So the meeting with Ava Chen went well, or as well as could be expected. The case seems to be resolved. Back to the grind of insurance work?" Stacy inquired, between bites of chicken and rice. Alan smiled with a glint in his eye.

"Guess who filled out an application for a Class C private investigator's license this afternoon?" Layla asked.

Stacy whirled to look at Alan. "Hey! You're not supposed to be snooping on my laptop," he complained.

"Oops," Layla replied.

Turning to Stacy, he replied. "Yes, I have decided to become a fully licensed investigator. I am confident that Dalton will sponsor me, and I believe the work I've been doing with Adamant will help meet the experience requirements. I'll talk to Dean tomorrow about it. I hope that I can continue to do consulting work for Adamant while also pursuing other cases."

"I'm in," Stacy said, then realizing she was taking an offer for granted, "Please say I'm in. Alan. I have to be a part of it. Insurance work is so boring after this case!"

Alan pretended to consider the request for a long moment. Layla eventually let Stacy off the hook, replying, "Of course you're in, Stacy. We couldn't do it without you. Who is going to save Alan when he gets into trouble?"

Stacy was beaming. Alan looked at his two partners, the enthusiastic assistant and the AI sidekick. This new chapter of their lives could prove to be very interesting. Whatever it was, none of them could go back to the way things were. There were dangers in the world that the three of them were uniquely qualified to combat.

PREVIEW

Enjoy this preview chapter of the next book in the Alan Harrison and Laya series: Cybernetic Resonance

I

A NEW ERA

The interior of the Screaming Goat Coffee Company was bustling with activity. Business workers on break, conducting informal meetings, or avoiding their offices filled the downtown coffee shop. Alan Harrison was engaged in two of those things. He sat at a table by himself, scrolling through emails on his laptop. A café Americano sat cooling on the table in front of him, and across from him at the empty spot was a café latte with almond milk. Alan was wearing jeans, a blue polo, and a charcoal blazer. A short blond beard accented his thin face. His blue-gray eyes scanned his email and periodically looked up at the front door, then back to his email.

In the background, pop music played softly, often drowned out by the buzz of patrons and staff calling out orders from the long counter at the front of the shop. Alan looked up as the front door opened and a harried-looking woman in her late 30s entered in a rush. She was dressed in conservative attire: a black skirt, a white shirt, and a tan jacket. She wore her straight blond hair short, just above her shoulders. Her bright blue eyes scanned the room. Seeing Alan, her eyes lit up even more. She waved and made her way over to him.

Alan motioned to the empty chair and the almond milk latte. "Good morning, Stacy. How has your day been so far?"

Stacy Collins sat down and grabbed the coffee, taking a sip before answering. "Chaotic! I'll be so happy when my replacement is fully trained." For the past few months, Stacy had been doing double duty as an assistant at The Adamant Insurance Group, where Alan Harrison had previously worked as a research analyst in the Claims Investigation Unit, while also serving as the office manager for Alan in his new role as an independent investigator.

"How is the new guy working out?" Alan asked.

"He's not bad. I suppose I was just as clueless at 25 too, but it's hard to recall. "

"So, I have news about the office you are supposed to be managing."

"You mean we can stop having business meetings at the Screaming Goat? Thank God! Where is it?"

"It's just a couple of blocks from here. Very close to your old job." He smirked at her.

"No."

"There is an empty suite on the ground floor of the Adamant building. I talked Wesley Jamesson into leasing it to me." Jamesson was the CEO of The Adamant Insurance Group.

Stacy groaned. "I imagined a fancy downtown high-rise!"

"Not on our budget, not yet."

"Okay, okay, when do we see it?"

"Tomorrow, maybe. They are clearing out the storage that was there. Then we can look and see what we need to do."

"Tell Stacy I said she is snubbing me." A voice said into his ear from the speakers in the Photonic SmartLens glasses he was wearing. It was Layla, his remarkable artificial intelligence partner. Layla had arrived one day inside a plain brown box with no return address, delivered by Stacy to his desk at the Adamant Insurance Group. Her entry into his life had transformed it, giving him the power and motivation to realize his dream of being more than a research analyst and setting him on a new career as an investigator.

"Layla says you are ignoring her." He told Stacy, who looked stricken. She scrambled to put on a Bluetooth earpiece.

"Sorry, Layla. It's been a crazy morning. I didn't mean to ignore you."

"No problem, girl. You have a lot on your plate," Layla said.

"What have you and Alan been up to today?"

"The usual, stumbling around a dusty fire loss, taking pictures, and asking intrusive questions," Layla replied. Alan nodded his agreement with the assessment.

"It pays the bills," he said, drinking the last of his coffee. He was really getting addicted to his morning coffee routine at The Screaming Goat Coffee Company. Yet another thing in his life he owed to meeting Layla. Their first adventure together had brought him here, and he hadn't stopped coming since.

"I am finishing up the report now. It's the Winslow claim. I'll send you the details for the invoice." Layla said.

Stacy took a pad out of her bag and wrote a note to herself. For the past few months, Alan had primarily done consulting work for his previous employer, Adamant, while handling a few small independent jobs. Building a business as an investigator was a journey.

"Anything else in the queue right now?" Stacy asked Alan.

"I have a couple of meetings with potential clients, but nothing solid yet. Something will come along. OH! I just remembered I got you something." He reached into his laptop bag on the floor and pulled out a small, wrapped, rectangular box. Stacy took it and, excitedly, ripped the paper off. She squealed as she discovered it was a pair of Photonic SmartLens glasses. They were a slightly smaller version of the ones Alan wore.

"Congratulations, Stacy, you are officially a member of Layla's Legion," Alan said, laughing.

"It's an honor," Stacy said. "Do you have to program them, Layla?"

"I've already reprogrammed them." Stacy opened the box and pulled out the glasses. She removed her headset and donned the glasses. They powered up with an audible tone.

"They are so cool! Thank you, both."

"It's our pleasure, hon. You are part of the team. And I need all the input I can get," Layla said.

"We have an appointment with one of those potential clients in half an hour. Are you heading back to Adamant?" Alan inquired.

"Yes, for a couple of hours. Then I'll head over to your home office and catch up on some of your billing and correspondence."

"Great. We'll see you there later."

Stacy grabbed her half-full latte and headed back to her day job. Alan packed up his laptop and exited the shop.

The offices of North Florida Aerial were in a two-story building in the San Marco area. The building appeared to be a former law office that had been repurposed for the startup drone company. Alan checked in at the second-floor reception desk in the lobby and, after a brief wait, the receptionist escorted him back to meet with Roger Maxwell, the company's chief technical officer.

Maxwell was a young black man in his late 20s. He was stocky, with thick arms and a crushing handshake. He offered Alan a chair in front of his desk.

"Thanks for coming in, Mr. Harrison."

"Call me Alan. Thank you for considering me for the job." Alan said, sitting down.

"Nice to meet you, Alan. I'm Roger. We've been in business for about a year, and we've just taken possession of approximately 150 brand-new, state-of-the-art aerial drones. They are essential for our new product offering to security companies that need visibility in large, open areas. Two nights ago, half of them disappeared. No sign of a break-in, no trace of them at all."

"Are they stored here on the premises?"

"Yes, we designated part of the ground floor as storage and a technical shop for equipping and maintaining the drone fleet."

"You've talked to the staff?"

"Yes, no one claims any knowledge of the missing units. Everyone swears they were in the warehouse two nights ago, and the next morning, they were gone. I need these units, and I really can't afford to replace them on my budget."

"Insurance?"

Maxwell looked a little ill. "They might not be covered under our policy. I am still discussing that with our carrier. But it would be better for me if we recovered them."

"My assistant sent over some rate information and a contract. Did you look at that? "

"Yes, the rate was no issue. We can sign the contract today, and I'll have a payment cut for your retainer. Can you start today?"

"Yes, I can start right now. Can you get me a contact in the warehouse?"

"You should speak to Ben Williams, the warehouse manager. I'll call him and tell him you are on your way down." He stood and offered his hand again. Alan shook it for a second time and made his way back towards reception and the elevator.

The warehouse floor took up most of the first level of the building. There was an extensive technical workbench where a half-dozen technicians worked on various drone models. Racks took up the rest of the space for storing drones when not in use, or on the workbench. At the far end of the space, a large garage door stood open. Alan could see two techs working with a drone in the parking lot just outside the door.

"Several of the units on the bench are the new Holliston 9000 series. They are very impressive aerial surveillance drones." Layla informed him as he passed by the bench on his way to a small cluster of desks between the technical and storage areas. A large, middle-aged man, who looked a little out of place with the young techs buzzing around the rest of the space, sat at one of the desks.

"Ben Williams?" Alan said to him, "I'm Alan Harrison."

"Good afternoon, Alan. Roger said you would come by."

"Tell me about the missing drones."

"They are the new Holliston 9252—the very best available for high-definition video surveillance. We just got them in." He nodded toward the workbench area. "The team is still getting half of them ready for deployment."

"Who was the last person to see the units here in the warehouse?"

"One of the techs finished working on one of them Tuesday night around 6 PM. He put the drone on the rack next to the others and went home. When I arrived Wednesday morning, two entire racks were empty. 73 drones in all."

"Who has access to this area when the offices are closed?"

Williams thought about this question for a minute. "I have the security codes for the alarm system, so does the head tech and some of the executives."

"Did you check the security logs? Was there any access between 6 PM Tuesday and the next morning?"

"No, the cleaning crew was here until 7:30. They activated the system. It was on until I got here on Wednesday at 7:15 AM."

"Could they have come back later?"

"No. They don't have the code to turn the system off. You can enable the system without a code, but you need one to turn it off."

"Has anyone talked to them?"

"I talked to one of the staff on Wednesday, and they didn't know anything. Said they didn't even come down here on Tuesday. They don't clean the warehouse every day, only twice a week."

"I'll want to talk to them. And I'll want to talk to the other technical staff. Can you set that up?"

"Roger says you will have our full cooperation until they are found."

"Good. I'll have my assistant reach out to you and set up scheduled times for all the staff. Can you email me contact information for the cleaning service?" He had handed Williams a brand-new business card that said "Harrison and Associates, Investigations," with his work email and phone number. Williams took the card and put it on his desk. Alan shook his hand and departed through the garage door to the parking lot.

In the lot, two technicians huddled over a drone. Alan stopped to chat with them.

"Is that one of the new drones?" He asked.

"Yeah," one of them replied without looking back.

"Are you having trouble with it?"

"We keep losing network communication." The tech said as he adjusted a cable on the rear of the unit.

"How often does that happen with these units?"

"Too often," he said, distracted.

"Alan, that is unusual. I'm looking at online records of failures for this model, and that isn't a frequent occurrence. I can't find any reports on their site that North Florida Aerial didn't submit." Layla said in his ear.

"How have you resolved it in the past?"

"Sometimes it goes away on its own, which is frustrating. Other times, we have to factory reset the devices and start over." As if on cue, the other tech snapped his fingers and uttered a mild curse. "Like that, the issue just stopped." The tech said, finally looking at Alan.

"I'm Alan Harrison, an investigator the company hired to find the missing drones." He said, answering the question on the man's youthful face.

"Pete Sanderson. Good luck with that. We have to get this unit finished and ready to be shipped out tonight." Alan nodded and walked off toward a dark blue Orion Chimera coupe. He started the EV with a button press, backed out of the spot, and drove off toward the river, heading to his house in the Riverside area.

ABOUT THE AUTHOR

J.E. Sutton Jr. brings over three decades of deep industry expertise in insurance and technology to the world of high-stakes thrillers. After 35 years of honing his craft and dreaming of sharing his stories, he combines technical realism with cinematic suspense. Living in Jacksonville with his wife of more than 29 years, spending time reading, obsessing over his NFL football team, and now writing..